Flint's Island

Flint's Island

LEONARD WIBBERLEY

Farrar, Straus & Giroux   New York

W18
C1

Foreword

Robert Louis Stevenson's *Treasure Island* was the very first book I recall reading, or rather the very first book I remember, for I did not read it myself. It was read to me by Sister Elizabeth, one of the Sisters of Wisdom who taught me as a boy at the La Sagesse Convent in Romsey, England. That was literally ages ago. It was before the atomic age and it was before the space age, to name but two, and it was before the television age, if a third be wanting.

I was perhaps eight years old at the time, and when I heard Sister Elizabeth read the very first words, I realized that there had to be a sequel to that wonderful story. You recall, of course, that most captivating of opening sentences: "Squire Trelawney, Dr. Livesey and the rest of these gentlemen, having asked me to write down the whole particulars about Treasure Island, from the beginning to the end, keeping nothing back but the bearings of the island, and that only because there is still treasure not yet lifted. . . ."

That sentence I first heard nearly half a century ago, and the "treasure not yet lifted" has haunted me ever since almost as constantly as the "seafaring man with one leg" haunted young Jim Hawkins.

I was greatly cast down to find, when the good nun had finished reading the book, that Stevenson had written no sequel and in fact was no longer among us. For two score years I waited for a sequel to appear from another hand, but waited in vain. The years went by. Boy grew into man, man into father, father into grandfather, and still the treasure remained buried and the island with its booming surf remained unvisited. At last I realized I must myself, however unworthy, attempt to supply the story of what happened to the rest of the treasure or die with that question, raised in childhood, unanswered.

There was no case here, I hope you will see immediately, of my pushing myself forward or eagerly volunteering; of hinting that what Stevenson could do I could do as readily. Far from it. I held back as long as I might, until the tally of the years began to mount to the point where the thing had to be done, if it was to be done at all.

I make no pretense in this work to being able to match the clean narrative style, the ear for speech, the insight into character and manners in which Stevenson excelled. I only hope that, having had to use three of his characters, I have not distorted them. Three? Four really, for in these pages you will find Long John Silver, Mr. Arrow, Benjamin Gunn (in a minor role), and the terrible pirate, Flint, whose treasure it all was. Stevenson paints Flint in *Treasure Island* in but a masterly line or two—the Squire recalls his topmasts sighted off Port of Spain, and the cowardly captain turning tail. Bill Bones, with the horrors, says, "I seen Old Flint in the corner there behind you, as plain as print." And then there is the panic of the pirates when Ben Gunn imitates Flint's voice as they plunge through the woods toward the treasure cache. Flint took over my own work without my willing it. He seemed to be always present as I wrote. I can truthfully say that when I started this tale I had no idea how it would end. Flint told me.

A word more and I am done. *Treasure Island* is essentially an English tale. *Flint's Island* is American in that those involved come from no cozy English hamlet but from the broader, starker streets of Salem in what was then British America. It seemed right to me that this should be so, for the lonely inn on the Bristol road is eternally Stevenson's, as well as the Squire's great house and the decent dwelling of Dr. Livesey. To have a second adventure start from such a scene (tempting as the contrast between rural England and the Spanish Main undoubtedly is) would be to push trespass beyond civilized bounds. Again, British America in the eighteenth century was the scene of much piracy, its sea lanes known to many marauders. Tew (Stevenson's Pew?), Kidd, Blackbeard, Lafitte, Roberts, and a score of others knew the colonial coasts from Salem to Port of Spain. So my tale concerns New and not Old England. This may offend some, but there is not a particle of nationalism in it. I have scarcely to remind the reader that Stevenson, who wrote so well of English inns and ports, was a Scot, and I, who write in some kind of Salem and of Savannah, am of the soil and air of Ireland.

Leonard Wibberley

Hermosa Beach
September 1971

Flint's Island

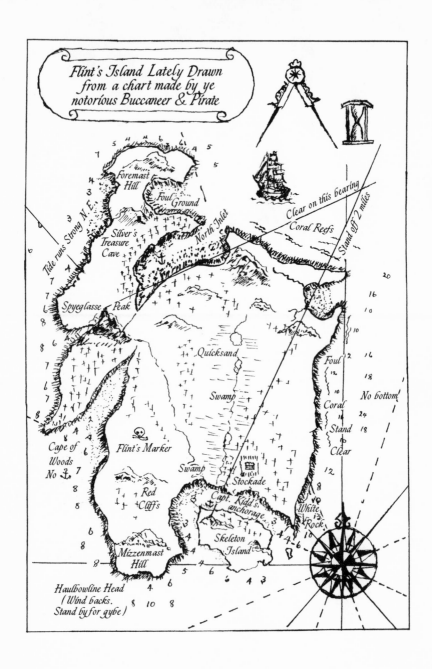

1

WE SIGHTED THE island at noon on the last day of August 1760. We had run east and south for a week before a series of unseasonable gales and were at the time many miles out of our way. The wind had a weight to it like cannon shot and there was nothing to do but run, Captain Samuels keeping what reckoning he might and remarking to the mate, Mr. Arrow, whenever they met, that so long as we kept off the American main, he didn't give a fig for where we were.

" 'Tis the worst coast in all the world, Mr. Arrow," he said just before the island appeared. "Not a light nor a town in a thousand miles, and reefs as soon as you've made soundings. I'd choose Africa in a hurricane to the American main on a thick night and an onshore wind."

"What can't be changed must be borne, sir," said Mr. Arrow and, turning to me at the wheel, asked, "What's her head now?"

"South by east, sir," I replied, though in the rolling and pitching of the brig, the compass was swinging three points on either side of that mark.

"Keep her so," said Mr. Arrow, and left the poop to go up forward to inspect once again the dogging of a cargo hatch that had threatened to come adrift in the forenoon watch. A fine seaman, Mr. Arrow; taciturn by nature, always concerned with the condition of the ship and the crew and seeming to have no life of his own outside those two entities. Nothing was known among the crew about him, though we had the fullest details on the other three of the ship's officers—Captain Samuels and the second mate, Mr. Peasbody, and Mr. Hogan, the sailing master—nothing, that is, but one aspect of his character highly peculiar among seamen. That was that he would not drink. This was vouched for by Adams, the cook, who asserted that when at the start of the voyage the owners had proposed a toast, Mr. Arrow had asked to be excused, saying that he had an aversion to hard liquor.

"And there's more there than piety," said Adams, who, perhaps by reason of a lifetime spent struggling with damp firewood, was inclined to take a distrustful view of everything. "Lost a ship maybe, or a wife, through rum." And this opinion came, during the voyage, to be shared by the entire crew, some of whom scorned Mr. Arrow for his weakness and some pitied him.

4.

Yet, in the matter of seamanship, Mr. Adams proved himself from the onset superior to every man on board, not excepting Captain Samuels, and all agreed that it was as much due to the skill of Mr. Arrow as to the captain's that we had come through a week of gales without major mishap. We were bound out of Salem, Massachusetts, in the Baltimore brig *Jane* with a license to trade in the West Indian Islands (Dutch, French, and Spanish) and as far south, if we wished, as Buenos Ayres on the Plate or Silver River in the Southern Hemisphere. You may be sure we were, then, armed with four long twelves aft and a bow chaser under a tarpaulin forward—an accursed thing that in the rough weather became constantly entangled in jib sheets and downhauls and caused many a bruised leg and arm among the crew struggling on the foredeck. Besides these pieces, we had muskets and cutlasses below, for in the days of which I write there was no ship met at sea that could be trusted. It was the French of course that we mostly feared, but the Spanish were known to be villainous and the seas in these troubled times infested with privateers of every nation, and pirates too.

Yet in the ten days since the start of our voyage we had sighted but one Portuguese that had come flying past headed west, her rail under and three tiny figures at her wheel. She was gone into the scud in a moment and thereafter the ocean was emptied of everything but the howling wind, the roaring sea, and the patient tortured brig, stern to the weather, as she fled before the storm.

Then Mr. Arrow, having, as I said, gone forward to inspect the doggings on the hatch while there was still plenty of daylight, climbed up the foremast ratlines to the topmast futtocks and, swaying about on his perch like a bird on a branch, looked carefully around him. To the north and east the sky was dark and full of menace, the racing clouds seeming at times to touch the tops of the seas, some of them several hundred yards in length, that rolled down on us. Southward and to the west, that is to say on our starboard bow, there was a little lightening of the sky, and it was in this direction that Mr. Arrow searched the longest. I saw him, after a while, hail the deck in some excitement, but I could not hear what he said in the confusion of wind and water. But in a moment one of the hands came running to him, carrying the captain's long glass in its leather case, and a sense of excitement spread about the brig.

Mr. Arrow clapped the glass to his eye and Captain Samuels came lumbering up on deck and hurried forward to the foot of the shrouds. He bellowed something at Mr. Arrow, who shouted down a reply which I could not hear. Whatever it was, it was sufficient to send Captain Samuels into the rigging, and several of the hands (for the watch below had come on deck) climbed to the tops.

"Birds," cried Sweeney, the sailmaker, who was standing beside me. "Birds, by the Mother of God. There'll be land nearby and quiet water tonight if we can find a lee to run into."

"What land?" I asked, more out of excitement than for information.

"Well, it wouldn't be Ireland and Cork Harbor," said

Sweeney, who came from that country. "Brazil, likely. But never mind the name. I'll take what land it is to get out of the weather. I haven't had a pipe of tobacco in eight days."

Just then there was a hail from the foretop, and since the man who hailed used the speaking trumpet that was kept there, I could hear him well enough. "Land ho," he sang out. "Two points off the starboard bow. One tall peak. Eight miles off, maybe ten."

The captain had now joined Mr. Arrow in the shrouds and spent some time examining the peak. I caught a glimpse of it myself when the ship heaved her stern up on a big following sea. A solid, dark, sugar-loaf peak, remote and even in that first glimpse somehow forbidding.

Mr. Peasbody, the second mate, a dark-haired man disliked by the crew, for he was fussy over trifles, came to the wheel and confidently announced, on one glimpse of the mountaintop ahead, that we were coming in on the French island of Martinique.

"Mount Pelée," he said. "I would know that peak anywhere in the world. It's four thousand feet high and we must yet be twenty miles off. What do you say, Sweeney?"

"Well, sir," said Sweeney, "it wouldn't be the Head of Kinsale."

"I should think not," said Mr. Peasbody, who had no sense of humor at all. "That's in Ireland."

Captain Samuels and Mr. Arrow now left the rigging and went below to consult the charts with Mr. Hogan. They all returned in a little while with several charts, the better to compare the appearance of the peak with the view, from various approaches, of the islands shown on the charts. None of these views, however, answered to the peak ahead, and the problem was all the harder to solve in that, having run so long on dead reckoning, we did not know our position within a hundred or maybe a hundred and fifty miles.

"I think we are out of the common run of shipping," said Mr. Hogan, who was quiet by nature.

"Ship's boy knows that," snapped Captain Samuels. "It's plain as sense that we are not among the West Indian Islands. There's nothing south of Trinidad but a few rocky islets and that can't be Trinidad, for that's a volcanic peak or I'm a cardinal."

"A solitary peak," said Mr. Arrow. "Could be Saba. 'Tis a notorious haunt of pirates, Saba. Nothing more than the cone of a volcano sticking up from the ocean, with the people living inside. I hear they launch their boats by flinging them down the cliffs."

"Saba," said Captain Samuels. "Now that's a thought."

"No coral there to speak of," said Mr. Hogan, "and not much of a lee either."

"No coral and no wood," said Captain Samuels. "The main topmast won't last another week, given even moderate weather. Red Carolina fir. I'd as soon put to sea with forty foot of cheese to set my yards on. I'll warrant you, Mr. Arrow, there are as many pirates in a Salem shipyard as you'll find in Saba, or Jamaica, for that matter."

Just then the lookout hailed that he could see land below the peak—another hill or small mountain, so plainly it was not Saba that lay ahead of us, and Mr. Peasbody's suggestion that it was Martinique brought such a look of withering scorn from the captain that I felt sorry for the man. "Martinique," snapped Captain Samuels. "By thunder, sir, I think you'd mistake the Rock of Gibraltar." And the unfortunate Mr. Peasbody withdrew to the waist of the ship to be out of reach of the captain's tongue.

Eventually Mr. Arrow appealed to the crew, many of whom had made several West Indian voyages, asking if any could recognize the land ahead. But none could say anything for certain. It was not Grenada, which has a central mass of mountains, or Barbados, which is low-lying, or Trinidad, which throws a knife-like ridge against the sky on its northern approach, or St. Lucia, which has two big peaks, called the Pitons, to the southward, or St. Vincent, which has a massive volcano northward but with nothing between it and the sea.

We were not at this point greatly disturbed, however, for after heavy weather and no sight of the sun for latitude, it is not uncommon for a ship to run upon an unidentified coast, which can remain unknown until a vessel is spoken or a harbor reached. No man on board believed that we had come across a new island which in the vastness of the ocean had up to that time escaped the cartographers. We were sure that on our nearer approach the island would be identified, and our anxiety for early identification stemmed from the need for prior knowledge of reefs and shoals which might lie about.

The island was soon very much closer, and a change in seas, which were now cresting before they had reached half their previous height, indicated that the bottom was shoaling. Mr. Arrow ventured the opinion that, this being the windward side, there would be reefs between us and the land, for coral loves white water. Soon we could see three lower hills between us and that great peak beyond. They lay roughly in a line running from southeast to northwest, the one in the middle being the smallest of the three. It seemed also that an inlet lay ahead flanked by these hills, and Captain Samuels, eyeing the area through his glass, growled that if there were fresh-water streams flowing into the inlet from the three hills we could see, there would likely be no coral in the bay. "But it will be no safe harbor in this wind," he added. "Only a lee shore and a mud bottom, and so poor holding."

The captain, having given this opinion, left the rail to stand behind me, and with a glance at the compass, not swinging quite so wildly now, for the sea had moderated, told me to alter course to south by west, which would bring us in, as he judged, on the south and eastern corner of the island.

The wind now changed direction. It had been north and east and it now veered westward. Soon the solitary storm topsail we had been carrying was flapping and up went our staysails, then our topgallants and topsails, and everybody went very cheerful about the work, this being the first time in many days that we had carried any canvas.

A changing wind, to a sailor, is a change of fortune, and it was the greatest pleasure to feel the ship sailing again, instead of scudding, plunging, and reeling before the gale.

10.

The gentle lift and splash of her bows; her easy roll, replacing the dreadful stagger of the past several days; the sight of canvas stretched clean in a "soldier's wind"; and the prospect of a night at anchor off a strange island filled us all with pleasure, and had anyone come to relieve me at the wheel, I think I would have begged to be left with it.

All this time, neither the captain nor Mr. Arrow left the poop, but stood together by the starboard rail, examining the details of the island as they came into view. We sailed at a tangent along a heavily wooded and hilly coast covered with pines or firs, and two of the three smaller peaks we had sighted had soon lined up on our starboard. When they did, Captain Samuels called to Mr. Peasbody for a bearing on them, but that unhappy man, who had returned from the waist, was gawking at the island and had not his wits about him.

"Northwest by the compass," I cried. "And the great peak north by west." Mr. Peasbody repeated the information, and then told me loudly to watch my course, which was typical of the man, for when he was neglectful of his own duty his defense was to pretend to find fault in others. We were headed for a point on the southern end of the island with beyond it a hill. The seaward end of this point showed white, and Mr. Arrow examined it intently through the glass.

"Breakers?" asked the captain, and Mr. Arrow said, "No, sir. Not breakers. White rocks." He looked about him, at the great peak and two smaller ones and the white rocks on the point ahead, like one who thinks he had been dreaming and finds his dream to be real.

"I believe I know this island, sir," Mr. Arrow said at length. "Indeed, I know it well."

"You do?" said the captain. "And what island is it, pray?"

Mr. Arrow's face was hard set as he replied, "It is Flint's Island, sir," he said. "Flint of the *Walrus*." And at the mention of that name, clearly heard by all around, a kind of fear settled on us all.

2

THERE WAS NO man engaged in the coastal or off-shore trade in those days in the American colonies, or living within a hundred miles of the coast, who had not heard of Flint. His was a name to strike fear in the heart of the stoutest captain, and the sight of his topmasts off the coast was enough to panic a whole countryside. We all have our childhood fears. Some are brought up to fear Satan, and others to fear ghosts. But every child in New England, I think, feared Flint before any of them, and if half the tales told about him were true, Flint must have been wickedness itself in human form. My own childhood, I being Salem born, was full of tales of Flint, and my mother had only to hint that Flint would get me and I'd be sure to be home well before dark, whatever the temptation to stay out and play.

I do not know how many towns and hamlets Flint had sacked and burned to the ground (often for sport, it was said). The list embraced the Atlantic coast from the Carolinas to Maine. We in Salem knew Flint well, for he had once, to gratify some blasphemous spite of his, sailed his old black bark *Walrus* into Salem Harbor, summoned the townsfolk, and demanded that they attend a funeral service immediately for one of his wretches who had died aboard, some said of plague and others said cut down with a stroke of Flint's own cutlass. My father told the story often. The funeral, he said, was held with the whole town in attendance and Flint presiding. The corpse, wrapped in a sail instead of in a coffin, was buried in the churchyard, with all compelled to shout "Amen" to Flint's horrid prayers. No help could be mustered from nearby communities. A horseman sent secretly to Mystic for aid reported that the whole community took to the fields on hearing that the *Walrus* was in Salem Harbor. My father said that on this occasion he had seen Flint plain, being nearby.

"He was not big," he said, "but under the average height, and as thin as a corpse. His eyes were hard as jet, and his skin, which was deathly white, had still a bluish tinge to it about the jowls. He preached a sermon full of hell-fire and quoted the Bible like a Trinity scholar. Mr. Wedscomb, the parson, said afterwards that he had every passage right to a 'T' and if he had not been a pirate he would have made a notable bishop."

When he'd preached his sermon and buried the seaman, my father said, Flint set fire to the church and then with-

14.

drew. There was some talk, when he had gone, of digging up the body and flinging it into the bay, for it seemed an outrage that such a wretch should lie neighbor in death to decent folk. But when it came right down to digging, nobody in Salem wanted to touch the grave, lest Flint hear of it and come back again. That part of the cemetery fell into disuse and there the moldering bones were allowed to lie.

Such was the story my father (now dead) had told of Flint. It was mild enough, compared with many of the buccaneer's other exploits. The list of ships he had taken would, I think, fill twenty pages. He'd died at last off Savannah, Georgia, some say of rum and some of yellow jack, and it was stated that even after he was dead none of his crew dared enter his cabin for two days for fear of him.

What happened to the *Walrus* after Flint's death nobody knew for certain. We had heard in Salem that two of the crew had died in a little English hamlet on the Bristol road in curious circumstances. One, who had been a mate on the *Walrus* and had the appropriate name of Bones, fell dead in an inn in which he was staying; his death being due to a stroke. Another, a blind man by the name of Pew, was run over by a coach near the same inn. Rumor had it that the *Walrus*'s crew had found Bones at the inn and were determined to get from him a chart showing the location of an island on which Flint had buried his treasure. There was a story that a ship had been fitted out in Bristol, England, later and had found the island and the treasure, the name of the ship being given as the *Hispaniola*. Whether that was true or not, I could not say. But there was no doubt in any-

15.

body's mind that Flint had had vast treasure when he died, and had buried it, either on an uncharted island or, more likely, on one of the small uninhabited islands of the West Indies visited occasionally by whalers in search of fresh water or goat meat.

When, then, Mr. Arrow said that the island now lying before us was Flint's Island, every head turned to look at it, the faces a study between fear of Flint and thoughts of treasure. Captain Samuels bellowed to the hands to get about their business and set Mr. Peasbody sharply forward with orders to put a good hand in the chains with a lead line. But he was himself shaken by Mr. Arrow's news and I watched him, out of the corner of my eye, staring at the island as we neared that point with the white rocks, debating, as I thought, whether we should sheer off or put in for a rest and repairs.

"Is there an anchorage in the lee beyond that point, Mr. Arrow?" he asked.

"Yes, sir, there is," said the mate. "That hill you see beyond the point is Skeleton Island. There is a passage running roughly north-northwest between it and the point, with three fathoms clear in the center. We can come in there if the wind will hold, and anchor in quiet water between Skeleton Island and the main, or Flint's, Island. The bottom is mud and sand, the mud above and the sand half a fathom below. It is good holding ground and is called Captain Kidd's Anchorage."

The captain received this information with some distaste. "Skeleton Island," he said. "Captain Kidd's Anchorage.

16.

There's not much that's wholesome in that. Were you long ashore when you visited here, Mr. Arrow?" The manner in which he put this question hinted that he suspected there was something more than a casual call for water in the mate's visit to the island.

"You mistake me," said Mr. Arrow. "I was never here before. The knowledge I have of the island comes only from a chart which I saw once and which I had good reason to study."

"An Admiralty chart, sir?" asked the captain.

"No, sir," said Mr. Arrow. "Not an Admiralty chart." But he offered nothing further.

"What is the name of the big peak?" asked the captain.

"Spyglass," said Mr. Arrow. "The one to the north, which is lower, is called Foremast, and there is one to the south which we should see shortly, called Mizzenmast."

"Hmmmmmmm," said the captain. "Named by a seaman for sure, and not a Spaniard. A Don would have used the names of saints."

"A seaman indeed," said Mr. Arrow. "And an English-man, I regret to say." Their eyes met, but Mr. Arrow said nothing more. Just at that moment the hand in the chains called out, "By the deep, seven," and then, "By the mark, six," indicating that the bottom was shoaling fast.

"Bring her in then, Mr. Arrow," said the captain.

"Aye, aye, sir," said the mate. "I should like to have top-sail set, for the wind will turn light at the point."

"Make it so," said Captain Samuels, and the hands were soon aloft setting the new canvas. The wind did indeed turn when we got the point abeam, and lighter still when, in answer to Mr. Arrow's order, I spun the wheel to starboard, to go up the channel between Skeleton Island and Flint's Island.

"Watch for a squall when we are past the point," said Mr. Arrow to me. The water about was entirely quiet now and I could hear the mutter of the ripples under her forefoot as the *Jane* slipped up the channel. The squall came as Mr. Arrow had predicted—a sudden little fury of wind which filled the topsails tight as drums and heeled the brig over on her side, very pretty like a girl at a dance. I fell off a little and then brought her up to the edge of the wind again and she slipped along as graceful as a swan. Even Mr. Arrow smiled to see her handle so well, and said, without turning his head, "Prettily done," which greatly pleased me. We had weathered the point at but three knots, but the squall gave us a good five and we sent a bow and quarter-wave out to lap on the shore on either side. Soon the wind died altogether and we lost way rather faster than I had expected.

"There's a stream runs out of that little bay there," said Mr. Arrow in explanation. "We are breasting the current. Mr. Peasbody, square the yards if you please. Bosun, is the bower rigged?"

"It is, sir," said Hodge, the bosun. "And I've a man on the cathead ready to let go."

We had soon come almost to a standstill and Mr. Arrow glanced at Captain Samuels. The captain strode to the side, looked about at the land to see whether we were still moving ahead. I could feel the wheel go slack, and Captain Samuels said, "You may anchor when you are ready."

"Let her go then," said Mr. Arrow, and turning to me, "She will come back on her hook. See you reverse your helm and keep her as straight as you may." There was a mighty splash from up forward and the thunder of the cable as it came out of its tier and through the hawse. "Give her twenty fathoms, bosun," said Mr. Arrow, and when that much had run through, a turn was taken around the windlass and the ship held fast.

I dropped my hands from the wheel and looked around. Dead ahead was a dismal-looking marsh through which a sluggish river wound into the anchorage. To the left of the river was a pine-clad hill, with one steep cliff showing like a yellow slash among the green. To the right of the river, the land was lower, though still rolling and studded here and there with pines and evergreen oaks.

Behind us, a battered skull as it were, thrusting out of the water, was Skeleton Island, covered with low scrub and with many rocks coated with bird lime. Three pelicans in a military line glided down the quiet bay, disappeared under the bowsprit, and then soared effortlessly over to Skeleton Island to perch on the rocks. Over the whole—the water, the pine-clad hill, the fetid marsh, and the oaks—there hung a brooding, menacing silence.

"I'd sooner be in Arctic ice with winter coming on than in this place," growled Captain Samuels. "Mr. Arrow, if you please, there are a few questions I want to ask you." And he led the way to his cabin.

19.

3

THE IMMEDIATE RESULTS OF the conference between Captain Samuels and Mr. Arrow, which lasted the
better part of an hour, was that we set an anchor watch
that night—two men forward by the bower, two in the
waist, and two aft by the wheel. All had muskets and cutlasses, and orders to report the slightest disturbance heard
ashore or around the ship. Captain Samuels made no bones
about the reasons for so vigilant a watch.

"I'm told by Mr. Arrow," he said, having summoned all
hands to the waist, "that the island we are lying off of was
discovered by the notorious buccaneer Flint of the *Walrus*,
now gone to his reward, and burning hot, I hope. It is unknown on any Admiralty charts, but Mr. Arrow says that
when in private English service he once had occasion to

study a chart (without latitude or longitude) detailing all the appearances of the island and this very bay in which we are now anchored. He assures me that this is the same island.

"Now these are unhealthy waters. You would not be seamen if you did not know that. They are pirate waters and we are anchored off what I might call a pirate island. It is probably uninhabited. Whether that is so or not, we will discover tomorrow. Meanwhile, good seamanship demands that I take the view that it is inhabited and inhabited by the kind of scum who have, in the past, using small boats, seized many an unsuspecting vessel. It is my belief that no ship was ever lost to buccaneers but through lack of caution on the part of its captain and its crew. Therefore, there will be a double watch tonight, and armed, and if anything is seen to set out from the shore, if it is nothing more than a sea lion, it is to be reported immediately. If there is any unusual noise about the ship, it is likewise to be reported. Do not be afraid to be damned as a fool. It is a wise man who challenges and speaks up on a watch, and the fool who keeps silent."

With such instruction, you may be sure that the watch was very alert that night. For myself, I got little sleep, for the talk in the forecastle was all of the island and of that infamous pirate for whom it was named, and (more to the point) of the treasure collected over twenty years of burnings and sinkings which Flint had buried on it. That the treasure was still there, no one doubted, and when mention was made of that English ship, the *Hispaniola*, which was reported to have found the treasure, everyone hastened to discountenance the story, though quite without reason.

One of the foremost in discounting the tale was the ship's carpenter, Smigley. It is an old saying in New England that it is a poor carpenter or a great fool who takes service at sea. Smigley, though a good carpenter, was indeed something of a fool. He was very slow in his speech and in his movements, and once he had set his mind upon anything, he could by no means be dissuaded from it. I heard Mr. Arrow say once of him that if he decided to whet the blade of his plane, he would do so though the ship was sinking and the water up to his workbench. He had round features in a round head— that is to say, the end of his nose was round and his mouth was round and his eyes were round and somewhat small, and it was a common joke among the hands to ask Smigley for a loan of his head with which to draw a circle.

Smigley then took it into his mind to say that all the treasure had not been taken off Flint's Island by the English ship, and he stuck to this view with the greatest air of authority whenever an opposite view was advanced.

"Well," I said at last, nettled by these constant denials, "how could you know the truth of the matter? You were never on this island before, nor ever in England to my knowledge for that matter."

"Well, I *do* know, Tom Whelan," said Smigley, "and just because you're quartermaster aboard doesn't give you any reason for speaking against me. You were wrong about the larboard channels and you should bear that in mind before crossing a ship's carpenter that's been at sea ten years before you were born."

It was typical of the old fool to bring up the larboard channels, which I had one day remarked were made of greenheart, only to have Smigley prove that they were of white oak. He would remember and treasure that error on my part to his dying day.

"Never mind the larboard channels," said the bosun, Hodge. "What do *you* know about Flint's treasure that makes you so sure it's still here?"

"Why," said Smigley, "I sailed with one of Flint's hands once. And he told me that there was treasure still on the island."

"You did?" said Sweeney. "What was his name?"

"Gunn," said Smigley. "Benjamin Gunn. And a proper fool he were too. Kind of sly and simple at the same time. Never asked you a question straight out but come at it first this way and then that, like a cat with a pine shaving. Well, he'd been on that same ship you're talking about, Mr. Tom Whelan, when they got the treasure. In fact, it was he who found it, for he had been marooned on the island some years before the English ship arrived. And he said there was treasure still unlifted there—great bars of silver, he said. And jewels too that he knowed about—crosses of gold set with emeralds and rubies and them blue stones that I misremember how they are named."

"Diamond," said someone.

"Diamonds is white," said Smigley with great scorn. "I

23.

seen a diamond once and I wouldn't know it from a piece of glass."

"And how do you know it wasn't a piece of glass?" said one of the younger hands.

"Would a Spanish bishop be walking around with a piece of glass in a ring, big enough to put in a bull's nose?" demanded Smigley, and that settled that.

"Tell us more about this here Benjamin Gunn," said Hodge. "If he was on the island and marooned and found the treasure and handed it I suppose over to the captain of that English ship, it's likely he got a good share, didn't he?"

"He did," said Smigley.

"Then how did you meet him at sea?" demanded Hodge. "There's no man will take ship who has half a George in his pocket. Poverty makes seamen. That's known."

"Well," said Smigley, "there's some you can give a dollar and they will have it in their hand the day they die, and there's some you can give a king's ransom and they will be looking for a loan Monday week. And that was the way with Benjamin Gunn. He had no sooner got back to Bristol than he took a coach to London and placed orders with every hatter, wigmaker, and tailor in the town. He ordered a coach and six, japanned in red enamel and with the spokes of the wheels covered with gold leaf. He was most particular about that. He hired a great house with servants that helped themselves, and met a duke in a tavern, with his duchess, that took him to their London home to introduce him to their fine daughter. Between the duke and the coach and the great house and the servants, and the wigmakers, and a few hands at cards, he was walking back to Bristol in three weeks without a penny in his pocket and the bailiffs looking for him."

"Good luck to him," said Green, the younger hand who had spoken up before. "Easy come and easy go, I say. It's not every seaman has a chance of a fling in London with a duke's daughter."

"I'll say this about you, young Green," said Smigley, "you'll either change your tune or die in a ditch."

"Did he tell you plainly that there was treasure still left on the island?" persisted Hodge.

"He did," said Smigley. "As plain as Benjamin Gunn could tell anything."

"Well, just what did he say?" demanded the bosun.

"He said the greater part of Flint's hoard was still beneath the ground—that's what he said," replied Smigley. "And that was as plain as Benjamin Gunn could put anything."

"Jewels, then—and coins?"

But now Smigley had turned sullen and would say no more. He had said quite enough, however. The forecastle could talk of nothing but treasure and what would likely be each man's share (for the poor fools did not doubt for a moment but that they would start looking for it tomorrow and immediately find it). I suspect that half a dozen coaches, japanned in red enamel, were rolling about the forecastle in men's dreams that night, and seamen whose gums were black with tobacco juice were courting the daughters of dukes, for if there were not a great many

Benjamin Gunns in the world, seamen would be hard to come by.

My own watch that night was from two to six in the morning, and the moon, a huge golden orb, bright as a guinea piece but big as a wheel, was low on the horizon when I came on deck. It had sunk in half an hour, but the sky was adazzle with stars, only obscured here and there by rags of cloud. It was plain then that we had seen the end of the gales for a while. By starlight, it was possible to see the outline of the island against the sky, and even here and there the glimmer of a stretch of sand among the pines and oaks ashore. There was not a light or a movement on the island during my watch, but the occasional jump of fish about the ship was enough to keep me alert. In the quiet and the heavy tropical air, I had a hard time staying awake and indeed dozed off for a moment, to be awakened by Green, who shared the watch with me, asking whether I didn't smell something strange in the air.

"Like what?" I asked him.

"Smoke," he said. "Wood smoke. I fancy I get a whiff of it every now and again from the shore. You don't smell it yourself?"

To tell the truth, I couldn't say whether I did or I didn't, for it has always been with me that you have but to suggest that there is something in the air and my imagination will lead me to believe that indeed there is. But I said I couldn't, and when next Green spoke, it was to ask me whether silver was half as precious as gold or only one-third,

26.

and whether diamonds were more valuable than emeralds, so it was easy to see where his mind was running.

The next morning, however, there was no treasure hunting or exploring of the island, but only hard work of the most tedious kind under a pitiless sun. At first light, which came at six, all hands were roused out and the ship given a clean sweep fore and aft while breakfast was readied by the cook and his boy.

Then the greater part of us were told off under Mr. Hogan to stow cargo which had shifted during the gales, while Smigley was sent ashore with two hands (both armed) to look about for wood with which to replace our strained main-topmast and the fore-topgallant yard, which had proved to be rotten about the slings.

Another party, also armed, went ashore to replenish our water, and everyone had orders to remain at all times in plain sight of the ship. For myself, I was unlucky enough to be among those detailed to stowing cargo. I worked all morning in the heat of the main hold, the sweat pouring off me in rivers. Heaving crates and barrels about with handspikes in the close area of the cargo hold, I had no time for thoughts of treasure or indeed of pirates.

By midafternoon, however, all had been done to Mr. Hogan's satisfaction, and Smigley returned, very hot and in a bad temper, to report that he had been stung by bees as big as birds and there wasn't a tree ashore suited in his opinion to be brought on board the ship.

Captain Samuels was beside himself at this report. Whatever anybody else thought about treasure, he was plainly anxious to get away from the island at the first possible moment. He reckoned to have the ship ready for sea by the following day. To be told now by Smigley after six hours ashore that he hadn't found a stick of wood worth cutting was more than the captain could stand.

"Why, man," he cried, "I can see four topmasts from where I stand upon this deck. Four of them." And he pointed out four pines which from that distance certainly looked as though they would serve the purpose.

But Smigley shook his head. "Full of pitch," he said. "There's a pint of pitch for a foot of wood, and it won't serve. Need mountain pine, and 'tis the wrong season for cutting them, anyway."

"I suppose," said Captain Samuels with heavy sarcasm, "that I should go away and come back in six months."

"Are there no windfall trees about?" asked Mr. Arrow, cutting in to save Smigley from replying to the captain, which would have been disastrous.

"Plenty of them," said Smigley, "and full of termites. I brought back a sack of tinder." And he produced a canvas bag full of wood powder for the cook, which was the only fruit of his six hours ashore. He was so dull a man as to be quite pleased with his thoughtfulness in collecting the tinder.

"Sir," said Mr. Arrow to the captain. "I fancy there is still a place where we may get seasoned lumber for spars and topmasts."

"And where is that, sir?" demanded the captain.

28.

"There should be, beyond that ridge to the east, a small fort made of logs, and a stockade around it. I fancy there'd be usable timber there, and still enough daylight to go ashore and look it over."

"Take a boat ashore and see what you can find," said the captain. "You are to be back by sundown. I want no hands ashore after dark." Mr. Arrow looked about and his eyes fell upon me. "Get a brace of pistols and a couple of French cutlasses into the gig, Whelan," he said.

I turned to do his bidding, excited at the prospect of setting foot on the pirate island.

4

THE TIDE HAD begun to ebb, when we pulled away from the *Jane*, and threatened to carry us past the little point and to the west. I had then to pull harder with my larboard oar to correct this and, a hundred yards from shore, where the tiderace was particularly fast, had hard work of it. But I had been in small boats almost from the time I could walk, and at seventeen could handle even the most lubberly craft. So, with the aid of Mr. Arrow at the tiller, we soon got into still water, and with the sweat showing in dark patches through my shirt, I was able to take a little ease at the oars.

"You'll have pulled many a lobster pot in your day, Whelan," said Mr. Arrow.

"That I have, sir," I replied, for I don't think there is

a boy on the New England coast who has not had pots to attend at one time or another.

"Made of withes in the English style, I fancy," said Mr. Arrow.

"Yes, sir," I said, "though there's a few of the French kind being used, with the entrance on the side instead of the top."

"I know them," said Mr. Arrow. "There are some using them in Cornwall to this day. But they have a habit of hanging up on rocks and kelp."

This was the first indication I had that Mr. Arrow was an Englishman, or at least born in England. He was normally a silent man, but there is nothing like a small boat for dissolving the barriers that separate officers and men. I have often noticed that in such small craft even the frostiest individuals thaw a little.

As we approached the shore, there being only a very slight swell on the water, Mr. Arrow stood up in the stern to see ahead the better, and then steered for a little spit of whitish sand which lay slightly to the west of us. We had soon reached this and pulled the boat a few feet up the beach. There was a painter aboard and I took this ashore and, driving one of the oars into the sand, fastened the painter to it. I now had an opportunity of looking around. To our left was the low-lying area of marsh where the river flowed through half a dozen mouths into the bay. With the approach of evening, there was a shimmer of flies over this area and a sulphurous smell of mud and decay. Ahead, the land sloped gently upwards and was overgrown with shrubs and some kind of a vine which had small flowers not unlike those of the potato.

"Yams, I fancy," said Mr. Arrow. "And good eating too, if Smigley had thought to do more than condemn every tree on the island."

To our right a ridge, not above a hundred feet high at the point where its contour was lost in the undergrowth and pines, flowed down to the sea, thrusting out into the bay, to make a small peninsula. There were a few scattered pines about this ridge at the seaward end, and these grew more thickly inshore, where they mingled with live oak about a quarter of a mile inland. At that point they were too dense to see any farther.

"Come," said Mr. Arrow. "We must climb the ridge. The stockade is beyond. Give me the two pistols." He thrust one in his belt and hung the other on a lanyard about his neck. We each took a cutlass to help us cut our way through whatever undergrowth we would meet, but left the sheaths in the bottom of the gig. The bag of bullets and horn of powder I hung from my belt, where the bullets bounced against me as I walked, causing me to wish heartily that I could have left them in the gig too.

Mr. Arrow went off ahead of me, striding along so fast that I was hard put to keep up with him. He was, as I think I have remarked, of a thin and wiry physique, his skin sallow as an old sail, his shoulders somewhat rounded, and his arms scrawny and long. But he had remarkable strength and endurance and I was glad indeed when, about two-thirds of the way up the ridge, he stopped for a moment to examine two pines, close to each other, which had been struck to the ground by some sudden force, leaving their ragged, splintered stumps thrust up out of the undergrowth.

They were not big trees when struck down, being scarcely eight inches through the trunk. Yet it was surprising that these, out of all those around, should have been served in this manner. "What do you make of them, Whelan?" asked Mr. Arrow gently.

"Perhaps lightning," I ventured. "There was an elm outside Salem struck in that manner."

"Not lightning but cannon shot," said Mr. Arrow. He glanced seaward to where the *Jane*, now but a toy ship, lay at anchor in the bay. "Twelve-pounders, I'd say. These would be ranging shots. I heard Flint had good gunners."

"But if that was Flint's fort, why would he be firing on it?" I asked.

To this, Mr. Arrow made no reply, but turning suddenly, thrust on up the ridge. We reached the top in a few minutes but were almost halfway down the other side before we caught a glimpse through the pines of the stockade. It was a grim square of palings or stakes, about ten feet high, made of the trunks of trees all stripped of their bark and pointed at the top end. Long exposure to sun and rain had weathered them to a dirty white, and in one or two places these upright logs had been thrown down or stove in, so that gaps showed in the fortification like missing teeth in a skull. At one part the logs were blackened where an attempt had been made to set fire to the stockade.

On a knoll behind the stockade was a log house or fort

not over thirty feet square, with ports cut at musket height along each side, and a smallish door facing the sea. Between the fort and the stockade was a good hundred yards of sandy ground all around, so that whoever scaled the palisade was left entirely in the open with a large area to cross under the musketry of the defenders. Not an easy place to take by any manner of means, and indeed I could not see that it could be taken at all except under cover of darkness or by treachery.

We were still in the pines, as I say, when we caught our first glimpse of the fort and Mr. Arrow signaled me with his hand to stop while he studied the place. He himself went forward cautiously until he came to the end of the woods, though still some distance from the stockade. Here the stumps of trees showed how Flint (for it was surely he who had built this place) had cleverly cleared the forest from around the stockade as a protection against surprise, while at the same time supplying himself with wood for its construction.

Mr. Arrow looked carefully about before deciding that the stockade was empty. He had, it seemed, been impressed by Green's report of smelling wood smoke during the hours just before dawn. Satisfied that the coast was clear, he beckoned to me, and we had soon crossed the clearing among the stumps of trees and entered the stockade by its only gate, which also faced the sea. Out of this there flowed a tiny stream, fed from a spring which bubbled close to the rock doorstep of the fort itself.

Just inside the stockade, we came upon a grave. It lay

34.

on the left-hand side as we entered—a vine-clad mound with a scrap of board thrusting up from the end of it— not in the form of a cross, but merely a notice put in the ground for the edification of a passer-by.

" 'Job Anderson,' " said Mr. Arrow, reading the name burned into the board with a hot iron. "Job Anderson. Well, it was a good man that brought him down."

"Who was he, sir?" I asked.

"Flint's bosun, I think," said Mr. Arrow. "And as big as an ox. A good seaman, though," he added, and the re- mark was entirely in keeping with Mr. Arrow, for whether a man was a pirate or not a pirate did not affect seamanship in his view.

There were two other graves. The first was hardly good enough for a dog—a mere ridge of sand higher at one end than at the other, and not a marker on it. Instead, a few rags of clothing lay about among the vines, among them a sailor's leather belt with the brass buckle cut off. It seemed whoever was buried there had been stripped of his clothes before being interred.

The third grave was a little farther off, against the very wall of the stockade, and the name of the deceased was burned on a piece of wood nailed to the palings of the stockade.

" 'Thomas Redruth,' " said Mr. Arrow, reading. " 'Well done thou good and faithful servant. Trelawney.' " He touched the board with a kind of affection, and his voice was not entirely steady. "Redruth," he said, half in wonder. "Here's a strange place for such a man to lie."

"Who was he, sir?" I ventured to ask, but either Mr. Arrow did not hear my question or he decided to ignore it, and out of a sense of nicety, I said nothing further.

We went on then into the fort itself, past a little spring which bubbled briskly at the door. A ship's iron kettle, with the bottom stove, had been sunk in the sand to provide a well for the spring so that you could dip in with a pannikin for water. The soft iron of the kettle was red with rust but still served its purpose. I scooped up a little water in my hand, and found it sweet and cool, and the thought occurred to me that the last man to do such a thing might now be buried in the sand outside.

The contents of the fort were mutely grim, suggesting a fate as terrible as the graves outside. A rough wooden bench, with one set of legs gone, lurched along a wall, smashed in some violent encounter.

There was a rough table in the middle of the fort made of planks, and a ship's lantern with a lanyard through the ring at the top set in the middle. The horn window was so grimy it could not be seen through, and the wick turned to powder at a touch. One of the planks of the tabletop had been taken off, but carved on another was a skeleton with a glass in one hand and a cutlass in the other.

"Flint's mark," said Mr. Arrow, tapping this with his forefinger. "The skull and crossed bones was not enough for Flint." Flint's flag would have been well known to seamen, but it seemed to me that Mr. Arrow had an uncommon acquaintance with Flint and his crew and with this island. I held my tongue, however, and rummaged about the

36.

interior of the little fort. I found the stock of a musket with a portion of the lock attached, and a broken cutlass, and in a corner a mound of broken bottles. There was a hearth near the door—a flat slab of stone blacked with fire, with a shelf along one wall close to it and hooks below for utensils. On the shelf was a dark bottle with a cork thrust halfway into it, and beside that, surprisingly, a moldering Bible, in the King James Version.

Mr. Arrow examined this with interest and noted that a number of pages had been torn from it. "Pipe lights, no doubt," he mused. "And yet it's not like seamen to spoil a Bible."

"Flint's hands would think little of it," I ventured.

"Flint perhaps," said Mr. Arrow. "But not his hands, or I miss my guess." He nodded toward the bottle, which he picked up and uncorked. He held it to his nose and sniffed. "Brandy," he said. "I'd have guessed rum."

He put the bottle back on the shelf, restoring the cork, and then we went outside to look about for possible lumber for our spars. Most of the pine logs of which the fort was made had knots in them and were useless. But the corner posts were of clear wood, and in all we found a dozen timbers which would serve aboard the *Jane* handsomely. To be sure, Smigley could be expected to grumble that some were too short and would have to be scarphed, or that there was sapwood here or there. This wasn't the kind of lumber you could expect in a New England yard, but it would do in a pinch.

"Go on back to the gig now," said Mr. Arrow. "I will

37.

be along in a moment. There are one or two other things I want to have a look at while I'm here."

"Sir," I ventured, "do you think it wise to remain here alone?"

Mr. Arrow eyed me in silence for a few seconds. I do not know whether he was thinking over my question or was merely taken aback that I had been bold enough to doubt his wisdom. "I have the pistols," he said. "I will be with you in twenty minutes."

Off I went then, suspecting that Mr. Arrow wished to be alone with some dark memories of his past—ghosts perhaps which he could only exorcise once and for all alone in that fort. I understood his mood. Young as I was, there were yet some things in my own life which called for reflection and solitude.

I soon gained the gig, to find it many yards from the water, the tide being on the ebb, and I spent some time hauling it down the sand closer to the edge. At the end of this, Mr. Arrow had still not appeared. The sun was now within a few degrees of the top of the ridge and in a short while the greater part of the bay would be in shadow. Still Mr. Arrow delayed. I did not know whether to leave the gig and go back for him, or stick to the letter of my orders and remain until he appeared. I was still debating what to do, with as much to be said on one side of the argument as on the other, when there came a sharp dry report of a pistol from the direction of the stockade. That decided me. Seizing my cutlass, I dashed up the ridge, down the other side, and through the stockade toward the fort.

38.

"Mr. Arrow," I shouted. "Mr. Arrow."

There was not a sound in reply. I flung through the door and stopped, frozen in horror. Mr. Arrow was lying on the floor before me, face down, a pool of blood oozing from his chest.

5

THE MATE WAS beyond all mortal aid. I guessed that even before I turned him over. There was but the last flicker of life in him as I did so; a look of anguish and astonishment which faded into death. A horrid flood of blood covered his chest. One pistol was still about his neck on its lanyard, but the other, which had been in his waistband, I could not find. Lying on the floor nearby was something of far greater significance for me than the missing pistol—the bottle of brandy. The cork was missing, most of the contents were gone, and the air of the fort reeked of spirits.

While I was still gaping at the body of the mate, there came a tremendous whirring of wings, followed by several high-pitched and angry squawks, and a large bird flung through the door of the fort and, swooping across the room, settled on one end of the broken bench alongside the wall. There it commenced an abominable squawking, and through its diabolical screams, I could distinguish the words, "Pieces of eight. Pieces of eight. Pieces of eight." Then a voice hailed me from outside, calling, "Ahoy the blockhouse. Ahoy the blockhouse. Hold your fire. I am a Christian man."

"Who are you?" I cried, rushing to the door. Not a soul was to be seen in the enclosure between the stockade and the fort itself.

"Friend," came back the answer from beyond the stockade. "Hold your fire."

I heard some grunting and shuffling from beyond the stockade and into the opening stepped a powerfully built man missing his right leg and leaning on a crutch. He was dressed in ragged clothes, which, for all that, had the unmistakable mark of the sea to them. His britches were canvas. He had a striped jersey under what was left of a frock coat of which the lower parts hung in tatters. On his head was a bandanna handkerchief placed foursquare on his skull for the sake of coolness, and over this was a three-cornered hat, with the cocks all gone, so that it was sadly out of shape.

I have seen better clothing on scarecrows. The man, without another word, came plowing up the sandy slope toward me, laboring very hard on his crutch, a garland of vines trailing from the end of it, such was his hurry.

"Who are you?" I asked, stepping out of the doorway to meet him.

"Name of Silver," he said. "They call me Long John, and

41.

sometimes Barbecue, seeing as I'm a cook. A poor seaman shipwrecked four long years ago. I heard a shot . . ." He peered past me into the fort, and then his voice dropped almost to a whisper. "Hello," he said. "What's this?" And he started to back away from me, casting his eyes here and there as if looking for somewhere to run for shelter.

"He's dead," I said. "I left him here, heard a shot, as you did, and when I came back he was lying face down on the floor, shot through the chest."

Silver stared at me for a while, then moved past me to go down on his one knee, supported by his crutch, beside the body of Mr. Arrow. "Ah," he said, "he's slipped his cable and no mistake. No one to help him now but the parson." He sniffed the air and spotted the brandy bottle. "Well, now," he said, "here's a shift of wind and tide. Meaning no offense, but seems like he'd had a go at the brandy, as who wouldn't, says you, dooty done and none to tell him no? And what's this?" He reached beneath Mr. Arrow's legs and produced the pistol which the mate had had in his waistband. He sniffed the barrel. "This here barker's been fired," he said. "Barrel's still warm, you can see for yourself." And he handed the pistol to me. The barrel was indeed still warm and the smell of burned powder came strongly from it.

"Ah," said Silver solemnly. "There's a power of seamen died before their time from that."

"From what?" I asked.

"Spirits and gunpowder," he said. "I never knew the two put together among seamen without somebody's planks

42.

being stove. That rum, now. 'Tis nothing but a devil that men put in their mouths to steal away their brains, as the Good Book says."

I wasn't at all sure that the Good Book said anything of the kind, but this was not the time to gainsay him.

"What were his name?" he asked, looking at the mate sadly.

"Arrow," I said. "Mr. Arrow. Mate of the brig *Jane* over there in the bay. We'd come ashore for spars," I added, though there was really no reason for volunteering this information.

"Spars," said Silver. "Spars. Well now, I'd call that fortunate."

"Why so?" I asked.

"Well," said Silver, "if you didn't need spars, I'd be left on this island for many a year, and then again, spars ain't what I would have thought would bring a ship to this island. Not spars, mate. No. Not spars. And what did you say was the name of your craft?"

"Brig *Jane*, out of Salem, Captain Edward Samuels," I replied.

"Ah," said Silver, seemingly relieved. "Trading voyage, I do suppose. Mixed cargo all the way from wool to salt cod. Well now, mate, maybe we ought not to stand here agamming but get back aboard and report, sailor-like, to Captain Samuels."

"Yes, indeed," I said. "And the sooner the better."

"Now when the captain asks you how Mr.—what did you say his name was—?"

43.

"Arrow."

"—how Mr. Arrow came to be killed, it would be best to have everything shipshape. He wasn't a hazing man, Mr. Arrow, was he?" The question was put with a measure of slyness.

"No. He was a fine seaman, well liked by all," I replied.

"Ah," said Silver. "That's the way of it, isn't it? The best ones is the ones that go first. But harking back to what you're going to tell the captain. You'll be sure to tell him that I come up to you unarmed, and from outside the fort, and that I hailed you when I heard that gunshot?"

"I certainly will," I said.

"I been alone on this island for four years," said Silver, "and it would be a hard thing indeed to be clapped in irons by the first ship that called."

"I'm sure nothing of the sort will happen," I said.

"Well, mate," said Silver. "Being solitary has maybe affected my mind, for there's little improvement that a man gets out of talking to himself for four years. I can tell you that after a while words themselves begin to sound peculiar, when you say them aloud. Like they didn't have no sense. Now you take horses. You ever thought whether a horse looks like the way the word sounds?"

I replied that such a thought had never occurred to me.

"That's the trouble about being alone," said Silver. "You begin to loose your moorings. But coming right back to this here Mr. Arrow. There's just three people could have killed him, see. There's you. And there's me. And there's Mr. Arrow himself.

"Now you: you've got friends aboard that would speak up for you. Not that I'm saying a word against you, mate. I found you here with the body and I take as Gospel everything you told me. And so must they. Then there's me. Well now, Long John don't have a friend in the world. Not on the brig, says you, and not on the island either. And if it wasn't you that killed Mr. Arrow and Mr. Arrow didn't have reason for killing hisself—why, there's me."

"I don't know what you are driving at," I said, "but it seems quite clear to me that Mr. Arrow was killed with his own pistol and in an accident."

"Ah," said Silver. "Now that's a good piece you have on your shoulders." He put his big head slightly to one side and said softly, as if he were afraid Mr. Arrow might hear, "Was he partial to a drop of rum maybe—just a nip against the cold and damp?"

"On the contrary," I said. "He was dead set against spirits himself, though he had no objections to others using them."

"Why now," said Silver, eyeing the brandy bottle. "If that don't beat all. Wouldn't touch a drop, you say? And the bottle all but empty."

Just then, with a great whirring of wings and squawking, that same bird which before the appearance of Silver had flung into the fort and settled on the broken bench flew now straight to his shoulder. It was a parrot, a large bird, green, gray, and red in its feathering. It raised a gnarled claw to one hooded eye, as if in some kind of secret salute, and again cried out at the top of its devilish voice,

"Pieces of eight, pieces of eight, pieces of eight," very fast, and finished this exhibition with a series of noises very much like a cork being drawn from a bottle.

"Where did you get that?" I asked.

"This here bird and I been shipmates for twenty years," said Silver. "Him and me's the only two that survived the wreck of the *Hope*—that's the ship I was aboard as cook, out of Bristol with a cargo of finished goods and bound for Port of Spain when we struck. But that's a long story, mate. And, as I said, we'd best be getting back aboard."

Off we went then, with just enough sunlight to get to the top of the ridge. It was gone entirely when we passed the crest, and the twilight itself was fading into night when we reached the side of the *Jane*.

You may be sure, remembering the armed watch we kept aboard, that I hailed the brig when some distance off, and identified myself. When I reached the deck, Mr. Hogan, who was on duty, asked where was Mr. Arrow and what was the shot they heard. I told him that Mr. Arrow was dead on the island, that I had found the man Silver there, and was taken immediately to Captain Samuels to relate the whole story to him in the privacy of his cabin. Captain Samuels was a man impatient of trifles, but where weighty matters were concerned he could sit in silence until all pertinent information had been laid before him. He listened then, his face a mask, while I gave him every detail of the tragedy. Silver, leaning on his crutch, stood respectfully by the door, as if excusing himself for being present at all, and did not interrupt with a single word until my tale was done.

46.

"The treasure's gone, then," said Captain Samuels, and he sounded distinctly relieved.

"In a manner of speaking," said Silver.

"And what do you mean by that?" asked Captain Samuels.

"Why, sir," said Silver. "There was more buried than was took away. And I found it."

"How much more?" asked the captain.

For answer Silver reached in his ragged coat and took out a gold ring with a green stone set in it. "What do you reckon that might be worth?" he asked.

The captain examined it closely, holding it up to the light of the lantern and polishing the stone with his sleeve. "Why," he said after his inspection, "I believe you might get a hundred dollars for that on any street in Boston."

"Ah," said Silver, pocketing the ring and settling back on his crutch, "then the rest of what I found, I reckon, might buy the whole town."

6

CAPTAIN SAMUELS MADE NO immediate comment on Silver's statement. He stared at the sea cook, then at the table before him, and then rising, still without a word, stared through the ports of the cabin at the reflection of the ship's stern lantern in the water below, his broad back to the two of us.

When at last he turned, his face was a mask. "Enough to buy the city of Boston," he said. "That would be a very considerable treasure indeed, Mr. Silver. More, I think, than I could fetch away in this ship."

"Begging your pardon, sir," said Silver, "but depending upon what the treasure might be. Now there's bar silver in pigs weighing close on sixty pounds a piece maybe, and there's enough of them to ballast this here ship, and she carrying topsails. And then there's other things on top of that."

"Such as?" asked Captain Samuels.

"Well now," said Silver, "I've been open and square and aboveboard with you. But we're coming to short tacks here, and there's the matter of whose treasure it might be when we get it ashore. Like here on this island I reckon 'tis mine, since I found it and finders keepers was always a good rule. Ah, but how are you going to get it away, Long John Silver, you says? And what good is it to you here on this island? And you've got the wind of me there and no mistake. Now I'm just a plain seaman with no head for figures, nor for business neither. But it seems to me that now is the time to divide this here treasure and get it writ down on paper who has what share—all spelled out fair and proper."

"Well," said Captain Samuels, cool as could be, "aren't you presuming that I'm prepared to take the treasure off in the first instance?"

That really bowled Silver over for the moment. But he came back quick enough with a reply. "Why, so I were," he said. "But then I don't know many ship's captains that can explain to their owners that they'd come on a treasure on an island and left it there—trade being what it's like in these times, with cargoes hard to find and hardly a ha'porth of profit in ten tons carried."

"Why," said Captain Samuels, "there's nothing to prevent me taking you to the nearest port and coming back for the treasure, is there? I've the latitude of the island now and have only to run east or west along that line to find it again."

But Silver, though shaken, had an answer to that. "Begging your pardon and meaning no offense, but talking up plain as between one gentleman and another," he said, "you'd have sheep for a crew, and not seamen, if they'd sail from this island and leave the treasure behind. And I'd tell every one of them, down to the cook's boy, what's on that island and what riches he was sailing away from—riches he'd never get his hands on again if he were to live ten lives and nine of them ashore."

"Mutiny, eh?" said the captain. "You're a bold man, Master Silver, to hint of that in this affair."

"Begging your pardon again," said Silver, "but I made no mention of mutiny but just took the liberty of pointing out that you was arguing against nature. Now let's get to the point, for I never found it served a useful purpose to make four tacks where one hard on the wind would do."

There was a good deal more of this kind of sparring while these two men took the measure of each other, and it was as good as a play to watch them—the captain solid, grave, and authoritative, and Silver good-humored, persuasive, and sly by turns. I think Captain Samuels got the upper hand of it. The division was settled at a quarter share of the treasure clear for Silver, five-eighths for the owners, a quarter for the captain, and three-eighths to be shared among the crew. Silver, you may be sure, objected that the captain should have as much share of the treasure as he who had found it. But Captain Samuels pointed out that though Silver had found the treasure, he had found Silver, which gave him equal claims, and so at last it was all agreed. Captain Samuels wrote the whole thing up in the ship's log, signed it, and Silver signed after, in a very neat hand, I thought. A final clause read that the captain was to deposit Silver with his share of the treasure at Caracas, or the nearest port on the American main.

"I'd as lief take you clear to Boston," said the captain.

"I'll take my chances in Caracas," said Silver. "There's lawyers in Boston, and king's agents, and excise men and harbor masters and wharfingers, and though I'm an honest man, I know that that kind will get their hooks into that there treasure and them as gets a shilling for a pound landed will be the lucky ones. I'll take my chances in Caracas— no doubt you've friends in Boston can help you, but Long John, why, Long John's last friend is Long John himself."

"As you wish," said the captain, and assented to the clause. I was called on to witness this agreement, and Mr. Peasbody too. Mr. Peasbody's hand was trembling as he signed, for this was confirmation that the stories of treasure which had kept the forecastle abuzz since we reached the island were true. When he had witnessed the agreement, Mr. Peasbody almost rushed from the cabin to spread the news, so that when Captain Samuels gained the deck there was no need to summon the hands. They were there already.

The captain had soon told them first the details of the death of Mr. Arrow and then the facts about the treasure and how much was to fall to the crew's share. I am sorry to say that, sad as they were over the death of the mate, their elation over sharing in the treasure far outweighed their grief. Green was so flushed with excitement that he led three cheers for the captain there and then, in which Long John joined most heartily, and several hands offered to go ashore with the sea cook and spend the night at the fort, to see, as they put it, that some wild creature did not get at the body of the mate. I think they expected to be taken to the treasure there and then.

Capain Samuels, however, was not, as we had already seen, a man to be bowled over by prospects of treasure. Despite Long John's assurances that there was not another soul on the island, he armed the watch that night again and had six on deck at all times. Another man might have relaxed discipline a little to permit the crew to enjoy the prospect of the fortune that now lay before them. It would have been, to my mind, the better way to handle things. But it was not Captain Samuels's way.

Having set the watch, he snapped to Peasbody that the furl on the main and foresails looked like a pile of laundry fetched in hurriedly from the rain, and despite the dark, had those sails refurled. Then he gave Smigley a good dressing down for not sounding the ship's well all day. With everybody on the alert, he called me back into his cabin and told me, over his shoulder when I was scarcely through the door, that he was promoting Peasbody to first mate to replace Mr. Arrow, and I was to move my gear aft and take over Peasbody's little cuddy—a most uncomfortable little

54.

hole at the break of the deck, always awash when we were making heavy weather of it.

"You've nothing more you can tell me about that man Silver and the death of Mr. Arrow?" he asked me as I was about to leave.

I told him that I believed I had given him all the details, but he was not satisfied.

"It's the brandy that disturbs me," he said. "I've known Mr. Arrow five years, on and off, and I've never known him to take a drop of spirits. Not one drop."

For myself, I did not find the matter of the brandy so strange. My own father, now dead, had been what we called in Salem a "sudden man." He would be sober for months, indeed years at a time, and then one day turn up at home dead drunk, or more likely, my poor mother would be told to fetch him, utterly intoxicated, from some tavern or gutter in which he lay helpless.

There was no explanation for these fits. Neither good fortune nor bad fortune seemed to have any effect on their occurrence. They were unpredictable and were always followed by dreadful periods of remorse (which I disliked far more than the intoxication itself) and then, after a while, another long bout of sobriety, to be terminated just as unexpectedly by sudden and inexplicable intoxication. In the end this weakness had been the death of him, for staggering home one night, he had been run down by a private coach and was found dead in a ditch the following day.

I assumed that Mr. Arrow had been a man like my father,

55.

whose drunkenness came in unpredictable fits, as it were, and such a fit had come over him, alone in that fort with his memories—whatever they might be—and a bottle of brandy at hand.

Of those memories Captain Samuels gave me a hint that night. Strict as he was with the crew, he was always somewhat more kind with me. This was our third voyage together, for though I was only seventeen I had been to sea since the age of ten, in fishing and coastal and offshore trading, for after the death of my father I had had to take over the support of my mother and younger sisters and brothers. Perhaps my circumstances, of which he knew, being from Salem himself, made him kinder to me, for under all his harshness there was much humanity in the man.

"Mr. Arrow was no stranger to this island, as you know," said the captain. "He told me last night something about it. He had engaged as mate of that very English ship which was reported to have taken off the bulk of the treasure from this island—the *Hispaniola* of Bristol, Captain James Smollett."

"Didn't he say he had never landed on the island?" I ventured.

"True," said the captain. "He had not. He had seen the chart, as had all the ship's officers, though without latitude and longitude, but he was lost at sea before the *Hispaniola* ever reached this island."

"Lost at sea?" I said, surprised.

"Yes," said Captain Samuels. "Went overboard. Dead drunk. He confessed to me yesterday that he used to be a very hard drinker and was drinking on that voyage from the day the ship cleared Bristol. He could remember little enough of how he went overboard, only saying that he came out of a drunken stupor to find himself alone in the ocean and the ship drawing away into the night. It was not until dusk of the next day that he was picked up by a Portuguese bound for the Grand Banks. He put ashore at Newfoundland and, he told me, never touched a drop again. After such an experience, I could well believe him. So I find his taking the brandy strange."

I did not want to disgrace my father by mentioning his own weakness, vows of abstinence followed by his utterly unexpected fits of drinking, though now that I reflect on these, I do not think he was any more to be blamed for drinking than a man may be blamed for catching a cold. But I mentioned that I had heard of men who took suddenly to drinking after many years of sobriety and then recovered and were utterly trustworthy, until the next time.

"Maybe so," said Captain Samuels. "Maybe so. It's possible that that bottle of brandy stirred something in him that made him try the experiment of drinking again. There is no explanation for mankind, Whelan, none at all. We are a surprise to each other all the time. But I would be happier about Mr. Arrow could I believe that in examining the priming of his pistol while sober, he had inadvertently fired it into his chest. The brandy is too much."

"It couldn't have been Silver," I said. "He was nowhere near."

"A remarkable man, Mr. Silver," said the captain. "And

as handy on that crutch as you and I on our two legs. He must be a famous cook, with berths so hard to come by, and he handicapped."

That was the end of our conversation. It left me with the distinct impression that Captain Samuels did not in the least like or trust Long John Silver. I put that down to Silver's boldness in arguing with the captain about the treasure, for Captain Samuels was not a man to be crossed. Silver hadn't hesitated to hint at mutiny in discussing the attitude of the crew to the news of treasure, and no captain likes that word even whispered on board his vessel. For my own part, I thought this but honesty and frankness in Silver. There was no sense, as he had said, taking four tacks when one hard on the wind would serve, and I put it to his credit that he had no nicety in discussing all aspects of the situation, and held him a candid and honest man. In the days that followed, he was soon a favorite with all hands, and even Captain Samuels became a trifle less rigid toward him.

THE FOLLOWING DAY a grave was dug for Mr.
Arrow next to that of Redruth, and he was buried in an old
sail in the sand. I have never been so affected by a funeral
since that of my father. I recalled how but one day pre-
viously Mr. Arrow had commented on the graves in the
stockade, never dreaming for one instant that he himself
would soon be buried there. The uncertainty of life was
borne very forcibly in on me, and Captain Samuels's re-
minder during the short service that "in the midst of life we
are in death" struck home hard.

We were all saddened and sobered by the funeral, and
even Long John, who did not really know Mr. Arrow, said
his "Amens" with a sincerity that I found deeply affecting.

It struck me as especially cruel that Mr. Arrow should be

laid to rest on this lonely island with pirates for company, as it were, while one of Flint's hands should be decently buried in our churchyard at Salem. We put him next to Redruth, and Smigley fixed a board on the palings of the stockade giving his name and identifying him as the first mate of the brig *Jane* of Salem. So those two honest men lay side by side, surrounded by blackguards.

The other graves were, of course, new to Captain Samuels and the rest of the hands. "I've often puzzled over them," said Long John, after the service. "I reckon they were some of Flint's hands, though how they came to be buried I can't say, for the Brethren of the Coast, as they call themselves, weren't that nice. Unless maybe they was buried by the same parties that buried Redruth there. Of course, they could have been God-fearing men too. But then it would seem that a word would have been put over them to that effect—this being the kind of place it is."

"Anderson was Flint's bosun," I said.

"Was he now?" said Long John, all surprised. "And how might you know that?"

"Mr. Arrow told me when he saw the grave," I replied. It seemed to me that Long John was entirely taken aback by this news. But he was quick to shake off whatever was the impact of my words on him.

"Did he now," he said. "Did he tell you of any of the others that was in that crew?"

"No," I said. "Anderson was the only name he mentioned."

"And I wonder how he come by that," said Long John.

"Still, there's no accounting for the kind of things a seaman will pick up here and there."

"Whelan," said the captain, interrupting this exchange, "take four hands and Smigley there and start getting out some of those palisades. Peasbody—there's good water here in this spring. Take the gig and organize a watering party. Bosun, I see quite an amount of clear gum on those trees. It will make capital turpentine. See it is collected. Silver, are there any turtles come ashore here?"

"That they do, sir," said Silver. "But not at this time of the year. But there's good fish to be had by the point. You have only to throw a line off the rocks with a bit of clam meat on it, and you'll have all you can eat."

"Then you'll be in charge of a fishing party," said the captain. So we were not allowed to brood but all set to work, the captain himself supervising every operation so that there was little chance for slackness.

Left to himself, Smigley would have pronounced every stick of wood in the forest and the stockade worthless. He was one of those men whom nothing pleases and he demanded from this island lumber of the quality available in the yards of Salem, Mystic, and New Bedford. My own promotion did not sit well on him, so whatever I told him and the men to do he took to be a sign of swell-headedness on my part. It is hard for a seventeen-year-old boy to rule a stubborn, fifty-year-old man, and I would have got nowhere with him but that one of the others, George Tester, an easygoing seaman, helped smooth things over for me. When Smigley objected to a length of timber as useless and not worth the labor of getting down, Tester would agree with him but get it down anyway, and the other hands followed his lead. Smigley took no part in the work of taking down the posts, his own labor being confined to dressing them to size and rough-shaping them with a hand ax. He was surly and slow and tried my patience to the limit. Yet I kept my temper with him, and after a couple of hours of dallying and grumbling, he settled down to work and trimmed the timbers nicely so that I was able to compliment him on this.

"Much you know about it," he said. But he was pleased all the same.

We found several cannon shot embedded in the palisade—twelve-pound balls, Captain Samuels said, and out of this reconstructed a story concerning the fort. It seemed to us that there had plainly been two parties here—one besieged in the fort and the other on a ship in the bay, the latter being the besiegers. Those on the ship I took to be pirates. After bombarding the fort from their ship, we agreed, they had tried to take it by storm and Anderson had been cut down in that encounter. His own people would not have buried him, but the decent folk in the fort did.

What was the motive for the attack? The obvious answer was treasure, and there being, seemingly, but one ship, the whole affair smacked of mutiny by a crew which had included some of Flint's hands, against her unsuspecting owners and captain who had come here for the treasure.

Perhaps it all related to the *Hispaniola* of which Mr. Arrow had been first mate. You may be sure my mind was active on the problem and I decided to discuss it later with Long John, who, having been on the island for a great period, might have arrived at a like theory or one of his own.

Long John had, of course, given us all the full details of his own shipwreck. The *Hope*, on which he had sailed as cook, had been becalmed for four days off the Azores after leaving Bristol bound for the West Indian Islands. She had not picked up a real trade wind until three weeks out and then the wind was uncertain.

"Quiet as a thief at a hanging," was Long John's way of describing the wind. "Now here and now gone and then back again. Our dead reckoning was more prayer than prospect, as the saying goes. When we got the wind, off the islands, we ran on day and night, with a hand aloft and another on the bow to warn of breakers, though thinking ourselves well to the west of any land.

"We struck sometime after midnight. I'll show you what's left of her. She had the bottom ripped out with the first blow. The next swell lifted her up into deep water, and down she went in ten fathoms on a wild night. Had I two legs, I'd have drowned with the rest of them. But having only one, I had reason to think more about shipwreck than others and I slept aft in the galley and not forward in the forecastle. They was all drowned in the forecastle, without knowing what had happened, but I went overboard with my crutch and so was saved. And as for them on deck, I reckon they stayed a bit too long and went down in the suck, or the sharks got them. Not a man reached shore but me, and I've been here ever since.

"You can see her main-topmast housing and the end of her bowsprit in the lagoon now. But the rest of her is broken up, or coral long ago."

Such was his story, and I have no doubt it has been repeated many times before and will be many times in the years to come. When a vessel is suddenly wrecked on a wild night, the prospects of any surviving are small indeed, whereas if the danger is appreciated before, many measures may be taken which will save the greater part of the crew.

It was for me a strange reflection on the perversity of fate that Long John should have been saved from drowning through having lost his leg. One-legged, he alone had actively feared shipwreck, and that had saved him.

We spent, in all, two days getting our lumber from the stockade, filling our water casks (we had, it turned out, suffered a severe leakage of water during the storm), and catching fish, of which a great quantity were salted down and packed in barrels. They were a fretful and uneasy two days for the crew, all anxious to get to the treasure, which Long John said was safe in some cave up by what he called North Inlet on the northeast corner of the island. He himself did his best to calm the impatience of the men, with whom he discussed the treasure freely.

"It has been there so long a few days more don't matter, nor a few months neither," he said. "You shall see it in good time and have long enough to gape over it, I reckon."

"A wall of silver," said Green, whose mind since we reached the island seemed to run on nothing but treasure.

"Isn't that right, Long John? A wall of silver, six feet high, twenty feet long, and a foot deep."

"Why, so there is," said Silver. "But that's just ballast, in a manner of speaking, compared with them chests. Why, you'd think Flint had sacked the Pope's treasury at Rome for the crucifixes and beads and chalices and the like. But you'll see it all in time enough."

Eventually the captain was satisfied that there was no further profit to staying in our present anchorage. ("Picking turpentine gum when there's rubies ten miles from us," grumbled Green.) Captain Samuels then consulted Long John about fetching North Inlet, and Silver said it would be best to round the island west-about rather than tack up the east coast, with rocks and coral to leeward. "There's a moderate breeze most days on the west side," he said, "with a lee for three miles to seaward off the Spyglass. But the current sets northward and will carry you past, and if you don't haul your wind until you have the foremast head fine on your starboard quarter and three miles off, you'll weather the point on one tack and can run into the inlet with the wind aft and round up pretty as a bird."

"You have the pilotage as clear as if you'd sailed it yourself," said Captain Samuels.

"Why, and so I have, sir, in a manner of speaking," said Silver. "Many's the time I've thought about getting the treasure off of this here island and I've thought everything out, for I never gave up hope but that a ship would come and I wouldn't have to leave my bones here. I've had dreams about it too and often I've woke up in the night in a sweat,

65.

sure that a ship had passed while I was asleep, or was maybe just clearing the point. Aye, and I've leaped up and flung along on my crutch, a mile or two miles or maybe more, in the middle of the night hollering aloud like a fool in Bedlam, and found nothing but the sea rolling around and flashing white here and there in the starlight.

"There was times too when I told myself that if I didn't look at the sea for a week, there would be a ship there the first day I looked, making a bargain, in a manner of speaking, with my Creator. But two hours I reckon was as long as I could keep my eyes off the sea in daylight, though there's many a time I've thought that there is nothing in God's world as cruel as the ocean."

"You'd have done better to have kept a fire going," said Captain Samuels, cutting him short, and the remark, so lacking in sympathy, did not sit well with Silver—or the crew, for that matter.

8

THE *Jane's* ANCHOR came up with a will at first light
on the following day. The patience of the crew, with treasure awaiting them, had been tried to the fullest by Captain
Samuels, and I think even he became aware that this was not
the best time for picking pine gum, topping up water casks,
and replacing spars. When the order to weigh was given,
there were more hands at the capstan than our mud berth
warranted, and the bosun's mate had the pump already
rigged to hose down the big bower as it came up to the cathead. We had only the smallest breeze and spread all our
canvas, but the hands would willingly have taken to the
boats and towed or kedged us past Haulbowline Head, had
that been demanded. The head lay to the south, and what
breeze we had being northerly, we had soon reached it,
when Long John, with a quick glance about, suggested with

the greatest deference that we stand off a mile or two to clear the lee of Mizzenmast Hill.

"There's a bit of tide flows past the head inshore," he said. "It will run foul at this hour, but if we stand off a mile, we will be out of it."

"Keep her south then," said the captain to the helmsman, and then to Silver, "Where will we pick up the true wind?"

"As soon as we are a little over a mile off," said Silver. "It will come in at north to northeast, and between the Mizzen and Spyglass peaks 'tis a man-o'-war's wind and no mistake. There'll be enough I do believe to carry her through the lee of the Foremast, and then the same wind all the way to North Inlet, though dropping with the sun."

"And the total passage ten leagues, you say?" asked the captain.

"Ten leagues," said Silver, "and not a shot more. We should fetch North Inlet by high noon in such a craft as this." The compliment, suggesting that the *Jane* could average five knots in her voyage around two sides of the island, was not lost on Captain Samuels. "By six bells of the forenoon watch, if I could trust my topmasts," said the captain, bringing a hearty "Aye, aye" from Silver.

It was a pleasure to watch the man, now that he was aboard a ship after his years spent marooned ashore. His eyes were everywhere, traveling up the shrouds and along the yards, darting to the braces and buntlines and sheets, then to the stays and clew earrings and all the bits of gear and tackle that are the quiet delight of all seamen.

I do not know of any calling in which all of its members,

however humble, take such pleasure in its workaday trappings as that of the sea. It is not so, I think, with carters or with quarrymen, for I have tried my hand at those trades. But among seamen a well-made splice, nicely tarred ratlines and deadeyes, even the puddening on yards to prevent chafing, are sources of pleasure and much good talk. Silver, long deprived of them, took more pleasure in these things than any man aboard.

Since he was to be our pilot, he stood on the poop deck, normally reserved for the captain, the officer of the watch, and the helmsman. But he took his position to leeward and at a respectful distance from Captain Samuels. He had his crutch hung about his neck on a lanyard, and his parrot was perched on one shoulder, enjoying the breeze as much as its master. I had thought that Silver would have trouble getting about. But he was wonderfully spry on that crutch of his, and indeed at times at an advantage over two-legged men, for he would put it before him, the end wedged up against a ring in the deck, and lean comfortably on it in the rolling and pitching of the ship, while we at times had to reach for some handhold to steady us.

As for moving about, he sometimes used the crutch and sometimes with a quick movement tossed it behind him and pulled himself along with a powerful grasp of the bulwarks or rigging. This need to use his arms to get about had developed in him immensely powerful shoulders, and the calf of his one leg bulged almost as thick as a man's thigh through the red seaman's stockings with which he had been supplied from the ship's slop chest.

He was quite right about the weather. We had a booming wind between the Mizzen and Spyglass, when we had cleared Haulbowline Head. The *Jane* enjoyed the work. Baltimore built, she had a clean run from amidships aft and laid down a flat but boiling wake which told us, without a single cast of the log, that she was making a good eight knots. I regretted my promotion, which, putting me in charge of the forenoon watch, prevented me taking her wheel, and there was a touch of pride in Captain Samuels's expression as the *Jane* bowled along, heeling to the wind and sending a rainbow of spray into the air now and again from her bows in sheer delight.

We had run the length of the west coast of the island in a little over an hour and a half, and then having stood off a league or more to make one board of the north coast to North Inlet, we wore about to the larboard tack and, rounding the blunt-ended northern peninsula of the island, ran down to North Inlet with a following wind.

"Begging your pardon, sir," said Silver, touching his hat and addressing Captain Samuels. "She has too much way on her in this wind. Topsails and the forestaysail and nothing more would be handsome."

"Make it so," said Captain Samuels, eyeing the narrowing channel ahead, and I gave the order to reduce canvas and hands to stand by sheets and braces for further work.

"Not wishing to be forward," said Long John, "but I'd like to take her now, the channel being tricky." A nod from the captain gave him permission to relieve the man at the wheel. It was an education to see him there, propped on his one leg and a crutch, moving the wheel with his powerful shoulders, his eyes flicking about the binnacle before him to the luff of the topsail, to the water ahead, and to the landmarks ashore. Sea cook he might have been, but he was a master mariner too.

The anchorage in North Inlet lay down a passage with scarcely two fathoms between us and coral, and not more than fifty yards wide. The fate that awaited us should Silver misjudge that channel, or should we lose the wind at the wrong time, was clearly shown in the wreck of a three-masted vessel at the far end of the inlet. Only stumps of her masts now showed, and the rotting decks were a riot of creepers and flowers. Two pelicans were perched disdainfully on the ends of her bowsprit, from which vines drooped toward the surface of the water.

"Keep her drawing, if you please, sir," said Silver to me. "Keep her drawing if you will, for the coral would make a Christian out of a Turk. We must have steerage and there's not room here for a bumboat to swing on a hook."

I had the watch trimming sail to my order, and we handled the brig like a fishing smack coming up to her mooring in a dying wind. The *Jane* was a lady and daintily answered to all this attention. The last wave had been left behind when we turned into the narrow part of the inlet, and the water on which we now sailed was as smooth and as clear as a sheet of Venice glass. Whenever there was the slightest flutter of canvas from overhead, we trimmed sail; whenever the breeze stiffened or Long John at the wheel fell off the wind, we slacked a trifle, and so we glided over the mirror surface, where at times the bottom was so clear it seemed that we were sailing on air.

The sea cook was splendid in his handling of the brig, and when we were deep in the cove, with scarcely room to turn it seemed, he put the wheel to windward and the *Jane* turned neatly about with no more than twenty feet between her and the shore. We let the anchor go instantly, and as the wind pushed the brig's head around, backing her yards, we could feel it hold immediately.

"Eight fathom is all you'll need," said Silver. "And if a stern line was taken ashore in a boat and a couple of turns taken around one of them pines, she'll lie here secure until kingdom come."

"Thank you, my man," said Captain Samuels. "You brought her in handsomely."

"There was a deal of pleasure in it, sir, thanking you kindly," said Silver. Just then, one of the hands up forward serving the hawse cried out and pointed over the knight-heads to something in the water below our bows.

"What is it?" asked Captain Samuels, and I ran forward to find out. At first glance I could see nothing but the gleaming coral of the bottom. Then the bosun directed my attention to an area a few feet to the left of where the hawse curved down to the anchor, clearly visible ahead of us. And there on the bottom, with rags of clothing still clinging to the bones, were two human skeletons. One lay on the other, the grinning skull cradled in its mate's lap, a tatter of a red knitted cap still showing under the gleaming cranium.

"More of Flint's hands, I suppose, Mr. Silver?" said Captain Samuels when I gave him the news.

Silver, before replying, crossed himself piously. "This here island," he said, "has got the very smell of death about it. But who they may be, I don't know. Flint's hands is as good a guess as any, but"—pointing to the flower garden of a ship at the end of the bay—"they maybe were part of her crew. I've not been aboard her, for she's crawling with centipedes."

For myself, I glanced from the bones in the water to the old, moldering ship and then about our own trim brig, and a coldness passed over me. Flint's mark, which was death, lay over the whole island, and I wondered how many of us would leave our bones in this terrible place. I think the thought was common to the crew. They were quiet about their work, reflecting perhaps that they were not the first to come for Flint's hoard, and others who had tried for the old pirate's treasure had paid for it with their lives.

9

WE HAD TWO hours' work when we got ashore to get to the cave where the treasure lay. The cave was not far from North Inlet in a direct line—no more, I would think, than two miles. It lay about a third of the way up a small hill just south of Foremast on the northern peninsula of the island, but we had first to climb a steep cliff by a path hardly sufficient for goats, and then, reaching the top, make our way through a thicket of pines and evergreen oaks with here and there growths of thorns so dense that neither man nor beast could penetrate them.

Captain Samuels came ashore with the first party, leaving five men aboard under Mr. Hogan on the *Jane*. They were to keep a lookout and commence removing our ballast. Long John assured us that there was enough pig silver to ballast the *Jane* to perfection.

The captain and I took muskets with us, while cutlasses were issued to the other hands, so that, getting out of the boats, we looked more like a boarding party from a sloop-of-war than a group of merchant seamen landing from a trading brig. The more able-bodied men were soon on the cliff top, and amused themselves with hallooing and shouting like boys on a picnic, while the captain and Long John plowed slowly upwards. Long John looked askance at the arms, for he had assured us there was not another soul on the island but himself. Yet it was not unreasonable for the men to be armed. These were uncertain waters. War might have been declared with France or Spain the day after we sailed. Flint was by no means the only pirate to cruise the Caribbean. If Captain Samuels had a middle name, it might well have been "Caution," and he was living proof of the truth of the New England saying that there are no reckless *old* sea captains—only reckless young ones, and they soon dead, or converts to caution.

The party at the top had to await the arrival of Long John before they could go on, and when he reached the summit, they paid far more attention to the sea cook than they did to the captain, which brought many a snort of contempt from Captain Samuels. But Long John had become the most important man among us, and I never met a man who could influence men so readily as the sea cook. The secret lay in more than his good humor, his willingness, and the skill with which, one-legged, he handled himself in every situation. In addition to these, he seemed to have a personal regard for every one of the crew. He never passed one of them without a cheery word, and if he had a favorite I think it was the young seaman Green, who was his constant companion. Nor was he for a moment neglectful of Captain Samuels, who did not endear himself to the crew by his evident dislike, for no reason any of us could discover, of the sea cook.

"Not far now, sir," Long John said when we had all reached the woods at the cliff top. "An hour and we'll be there, and even in the heat of the day the cave itself is cool."

The captain, who was sweating like a bull, grunted. He had up-ended his musket across his back before getting into the boat, so that should the boat founder in shallow water, the lock would not be wet. He still carried the musket this way. The stock had knocked his cocked hat over his eyes and he fetched his breath in great gusts of wind. But he did not slow down for all his discomfort or call a rest when he reached the cliff top.

The trees thinned as we approached the hill on whose flank the cave was situated, and we came then to a vast acreage or savanna of palmettos—small palms with fan-like leaves, growing no more than a foot or two above the ground and spiked on every frond with sharp thorns. These thorns were tough enough to tear clothing, and this place was the habitat of large, gray-green lizards, which scampered away in clouds of dust on their hindlegs as we approached, their tails thrust out to balance their foreparts, and looking for all the world like small dragons.

"They're harmless," said Long John, "and eat as good as chicken, but a little sweet, in a manner of speaking. Salt

76.

horse is more to my fancy, but then we always hankers for what we haven't got, human nature being contrary-minded."

"There's the cave," came a shout from ahead, and instantly the whole crew, with a loud huzza, scampered off, leaving Long John, Captain Samuels, and myself still toiling over the loose sand among the palmettos. They were all inside when the captain arrived, and the place reverberating with the hubbub of voices as he entered. Green greeted him at the entrance, grinning and staggering under a huge bar or ingot of silver which he had in his arms. "One for you, sir," cried Green, seeing the captain.

"Put that where you found it," snapped Captain Samuels, and Green shuffled off with no good grace.

The men fell back when they saw that the captain had arrived, some of them holding silver bars, others turning to put them down, shamefaced. They made an opening for him and he walked through in silence, I at his heels. Then he stopped and I heard him catch his breath at the incredible sight revealed to us at the back of the cave. There, piled up to the ceiling, was a wall of solid silver, pig upon pig of the precious metal laid like bricks from floor to roof and with a neatness that would have done credit to a master mason. The silver had not a high glitter to it. It was dark, almost leaden, but through this darkness the metal glowed with a soft deep light—the very soul of the silver, as it were, peering through its mask of tarnish.

"By thunder," said Captain Samuels, breaking the silence, "what a man was Flint." His admiration, viewing that wall of treasure, was genuine, and I think that from that moment he held another view of that frightful pirate whose name struck terror throughout the whole of New England and the Caribbean. I think he saw, beyond the looting, burning, slaughtering, blasphemous creature that Flint was, a great figure, capable of tremendous plans and daring assaults, of exact organization and immense control over his fellows. The treasure before us was the spoil of no petty action but of some great assault upon a treasure fleet or upon a city. Such daring, put to the purpose of patriotism and service of his king, would have made Flint's name rank with that of Hawke and Anson. Some such thought as this, I feel sure, brought forth from Captain Samuels that exclamation of pure admiration, "What a man was Flint."

"Ah," said Long John, whose mind was running in the same direction, "had he flown the king's colors, he'd be buried now in Westminster Abbey, an example to all honest seamen, instead of dying of rum off Savannah."

"I wonder what set him wrong," said Green, hoping by such a question, I think, to regain a little of the captain's favor. He was unlucky, however, for Captain Samuels turned fiercely on him and said, "The same thing that had you staggering out of the cave there with a bar of silver in your hands and a look on your face that would disgrace an ape. Greed! Plain greed. The difference between a king's officer and a pirate is that one chooses service and the other chooses self."

"Amen to that," said Long John gravely. "There's a power of reflection there. And Flint was an educated man,

I've heard. Could spout Latin like a parson, and write as good as a lawyer."

Beside that wall of silver at the end of the cave, there were four great chests in a kind of alcove on the right-hand side of the cave. The chests were reinforced with so many iron plates and bars as to be practically indestructible, and four bars of iron running through the side and the lid formed the locks on them.

They were not locked now, for Long John had had plenty of time in which to open them. He drew out the bolts, which fitted so well in their channels that they moved without any resistance, and threw open the lid of one of the chests. Even Captain Samuels gasped when he saw what lay inside. Diamonds, rubies, aquamarines, emeralds, pearls (both black and white), and sapphires and topaz lay about in profusion—in single gems, in broaches, in necklaces, in rings, in crucifixes, in bracelets, in medallions, in cups— indeed in every design that the human mind could contrive. Silver was all forgotten in a moment. It was nothing more than ballast compared with the splendor of these jewels. We stared at them, while the fire flickered on the cut diamonds and the rubies glowed like blobs of blood in the depth of the chest. Then Long John, shifting his weight onto his good leg and leaning against the wall for support, put the end of his crutch into the chest and lifted up a magnificent necklace of diamonds that sparkled like hoar-frost on a January morning.

"There's Flint's choice, in a manner of speaking," he

79.

said, holding the necklace on the end of his crutch. "This here, or Westminster Abbey. Honor or fortune, and he chose fortune. Why, with such a thing as this, a man could have the Queen of France sitting in his lap, and her daughters making him a dish of tea."

"More likely a dance on the end of a fathom of line at Execution Dock," snapped Captain Samuels. "That was Kidd's end, and Roberts's too, and Tew's."

"Right you are, sir," said Silver quickly. "And no offense meant, I'm sure. Many's the time I'd have given everything in this cave for the sight of a ship closing on this island. 'Tis a strange fancy, but I've had the feeling too that Flint himself was in this cave, watching his treasure, and there's been times when I was afraid to sleep here, being all alone."

"As to giving the treasure away," said Captain Samuels, "you drove a hard enough bargain when I came to get you. And as I've said before, you'd have done better to have kept a fire lit. I think there was a fine play actor lost in you, Master Silver, and if you run through all your money when you get ashore, you might turn to the stage for employment."

"Aye, aye, sir," said Silver with a laugh which was somewhat shamefaced. "You have the right of it there. But tending fires on mountaintops is hard work for a one-legged man, and after a while it somehow don't seem no use."

Smigley, the carpenter, was one of the shore party, and although I will not say that he was unimpressed by the jewels, the chests were what commanded his greatest admiration. He examined them with reverence, shaking his

80.

head and clucking his tongue, and announced that he had never seen workmanship so fine. "This here's Spanish oak," he said. "Through-bolted every two inches, and the ends riveted over the bolts. Them iron bands was put on hot and quenched like an iron tire to pull all in. Why, this here chest would withstand cannon shot. You could fling it, full as it is, from the top of them cliffs to the bottom without straining a hinge."

"Well now," said Sweeney, the sailmaker, "if I should wind up with the chests, I'll let you have them for a capful of diamonds."

Captain Samuels now inquired for the locks on the chests, and Silver said he had had to break these. "Well," said the captain, "I will have the blacksmith make locks when we get them aboard. Meanwhile, there is no reason for them to stay here another hour. Bosun, rig a sling from two poles, so that we may have four hands to each chest to get them to the cliff, and have a whip rigged at some suitable point at the edge of the cliff to lower them by. We have some hours of daylight and there is no reason why we should not have those chests aboard tonight."

"Aye, aye, sir," said the bosun. "Begging your pardon, the other hands might carry that bar silver to the cliff edge also. I'm thinking we could lower it down two bars to a load on the same whip we use for the chests. They'll all go in the same hold, I'm thinking."

"The silver may go in the main hold," said Captain Samuels. "We can use it for ballast. But the chests shall go in my cabin—locked."

10

THE TRANSFER OF the treasure took four days. The crew was divided into two parties: a shore party under Mr. Peasbody and myself, who took the treasure to the cliff head and lowered it on a whip (that is to say, by means of a pulley dangling on a pole over the cliff edge) to the second party below. This, under the captain and Hodge the boatswain, put the chests and bar silver in the *Jane*'s boats and took it out to the ship, where it was stowed. We kept, in all this time, a lookout on the top of the peak in which the treasure cave was located, lest any strange sail approach the island. The shore party on the second night slept in the cave, but we had orders to return immediately to the brig if she fired her guns. Everyone, even old Smigley, was in good spirits taking off the treasure, and yet there was a color of anxiety to the operation lest some French or Spanish vessel, blown out of its way as we had been, should come upon us.

Being of the shore party, I slept in the cave during this time, and Long John, who also remained ashore, did the cooking. In that office he was excellent, providing plenty of variety and always cheerful about the fire, though at times it must have been unmercifully hot for him. He would be off each day to get plantain or other fruits to vary our diet, but always refused aid, saying he could manage best himself and reminding us that Captain Samuels was in a hurry to get clear of the island. "Besides," he said, "there's few seamen would pick fruit that could be handling treasure, and I can carry plenty with a bread bag around my neck." On these excursions he was sometimes away an hour or two, but always returned with plenty for our party and some to send aboard to Captain Samuels.

Long John was exactly the opposite of the carpenter, Smigley. Whatever the circumstances, Long John would be cheerful and prided himself in providing us with fruit, while Smigley even grumbled at the weight of the silver bars, never pausing to consider that their weight increased their value and he should rejoice had they been so heavy that two men could not pick up one of them.

Toward me, Long John was respectful and flattering. Now and again, with a colorful phrase, he would support some decision I made, and his flattery was not only in words, for he was quick to respond to any order of mine, as if I were a man full grown—accustomed to the position

83.

of ship's officer. I grew to like him more and more in the days ashore.

Long John was a great man for yarns, and around the fire in the evening after supper he kept us spellbound with his talk of sea fights and landings, storms and calms, mutinies and hangings. His leg, he told us, he lost at Quiberon under Hawke, and he told the story of that great sea fight which had saved England from an invasion by the French, with the greatest spirit.

"We had a northwest gale behind us and a sea like the end of the world," said Long John. "We couldn't open our lower gunports for fear of foundering, and we hauled up on the French in the dregs of the day with topsails set and spars carrying away like twigs in a winter storm. 'Lay alongside and take 'em to leeward,' said Hawke, for only our windward batteries would bear, them to leeward pointing straight down into the water, we was so heeled over.

"Our first broadside ripped the bottom out of a French four-decker that had just rose to the top of a roller and down she went like a stone in a pond, taking a thousand men and maybe more to the bottom with her. 'Don't cheer,' cried Hawke. 'The poor devils are drowning.' That's the kind of man he was. Some swore by Boscawen, and I served under him too. But there was never a fighter like Hawke, nor ever will be."

"Was it at Quiberon you lost your leg?" Green asked, all admiration for Long John, as indeed were the rest of the hands.

"Aye, at Quiberon, and with the next broadside," said

the sea cook. "We took that broadside from aft, and it raked us from stern to stem. I was at the wheel and she dipped and rolled as the shot came tumbling aboard. Down I went on the deck, not knowing what had happened to me until I saw part of a leg that looked mighty familiar rolling about in the scuppers. But it wasn't until I tried to get up that I found that leg was my own. I'd have been a dead man but for the dark, there being no time in hot action to tend to wounded seamen, other than pitch them overboard, which is what marines is mostly for. But night came on fast and the marines started cleaning decks and found me lying to one side in a pool of blood.

" 'Over with him,' said one. 'He's done for, and no mistake.'

" 'Not I,' I says. 'Take a look and you'll see there's more left than was shot away.' So they took me down to the cockpit, where the surgeon's mates trimmed the stump and dipped the end in hot tar to help healing. I've had but five toes ever since. But to tell you the truth, if I got my old leg back tomorrow, I'd have to learn to walk on it again, being so used to doing without it now."

Long John got no pension for his wound, he said, though given a license to beg. He could get no berth at sea thereafter but that of cook. Though that experience might have made him bitter, he had a great loyalty to the king and a great respect for Hawke, his old admiral. But for lawyers, on whom he blamed his failure to get a pension, he had a profound distrust and even hatred.

"Of the two first sons of Adam, Abel was the honest

man and Cain the lawyer," said Long John. "And if proof is wanting, you have only to turn to the Good Book, where you'll find that Cain not only murdered his brother but talked God out of hanging him. Now, shipmates, you may think it strange that I bargained with Captain Samuels to land me and my share of this here treasure in Caracas or some South American port. But I'll take my chances with the Spaniards and the Indians before I'll take them with them lawyers that will be on board as soon as you've let down your hook. And you mark my words, them that sees a penny in the pound of what's coming to them when the lawyers are through with it will be lucky ones."

"Well, we've got to go back to Boston or Salem," said one of the hands.

"Ah," said Silver. "That's a fact. Well, I wish you joy of your share. But I know I'm going to get mine."

"We could petition the captain to put us ashore in South America too, with our whack," said someone. "I don't see nothing wrong with that."

"Enough of that," said I. "You signed articles for the whole voyage."

"So we did," said Green, "but there's substitutes, ain't there? You can sign off in any port if you can find a substitute. That is the custom. And double wages isn't an offer to be sneezed at."

"Captain Samuels will represent this crew ashore as well as afloat," I said. "You can rely on him to see that every man gets his share. So no more talk of South American substitutes."

"Captain Samuels is as fair a man by all accounts as you could wish to sail under," said Silver. "I'm not a man to say a word against him. Not I, by the powers," and he tapped his clay pipe out on his wooden leg with the greatest solemnity—Green looking at him in surprise, I thought.

The talk turned to other matters, but I was uneasy. Six years of my life I had been among seamen, and I knew that, most of their lives being spent upon the water, seamen have a deep suspicion of landsmen. Their suspicion of lawyers is the result of their experience with signing ship's articles. These articles, drawn up by lawyers, always seem to contain some clause that works against the seaman even when the clause itself appears favorable to him. If seamen, as a rule, do not learn to read, one reason may very well be that nothing that is read to them means what it seems to mean, but very often means the opposite. As for lawyers, many who go to sea have lost through some legal process their house or land or small shop ashore. Examination might show that these possessions were lost by carelessness or ignorance on their part. But lost they were, and there were always lawyers involved, and whenever a shark follows a ship, it is a standing joke in the forecastle to say, "The ship has a lawyer in tow."

This being the case, Silver's stirring up these distrusts among the crew was not something to be passed over without remedy. I determined then to mention the matter to Captain Samuels and did so when I saw him the following day. I even went so far as to suggest that he reassure the crew of his own determination to see they got their full share of the treasure when we returned to New England. But Captain Samuels was not a man to curry favor with anyone. He thanked me for my report, said he would have nothing to say to the crew, but told me to keep my eyes on Silver. "He's too nice for honesty," he said.

When our ballast had been dumped and the silver was all aboard in its place, I suggested to Peasbody that I take a musket and try for some of the mountain goats which were to be found about the island. He of course accused me of trying to get out of the remainder of the work, for the man had a meanness of mind that could not be eradicated. But I reminded him that Captain Samuels, as soon as he was ashore, had inquired for turtle, and was plainly anxious for any supply of fresh meat that could be at hand. "It would be a pity," I said, "to tell him we had not thought to get a goat or two while we had the chance."

"Oh, all right, Whelan," said Peasbody. "But take Hodge with you, and be back well before sundown."

So off I went with Hodge, striking inland along North Inlet to the point where it dwindled into a small stream coming down from the towering flanks of Spyglass. Silver was at the time off on his daily trip for island fruits. Otherwise, I would have been glad of his company as a guide.

Goat I reckoned would likely be found on the Spyglass, but when we had gone a long way up the flanks of that great peak, with the goat always well ahead of us, we saw below us and to the east a thick woodland with in the center of it a marshy area. Hodge suggested that we might find

wild fowl there, for he had heard some kind of geese cack-
ling overhead at night.

"We've bird shot in plenty," said the bosun, "and we
could spend the whole of the afternoon climbing the mountain without getting within gunshot of a goat. They're
skittish creatures at best, and the meat is too dark for my
taste."

So off we went through the woodlands, which here grew
out of a grayish soil, with not much undergrowth. We had
soon come to a swampy area of bulrushes, horsetails, and
lily pads, and here had good hunting, getting a dozen large
duck-like birds which seemed utterly indifferent to our
presence, so that after each discharge of the musket they
returned to the same little lake on which their comrades
had been slain. Two fell on a bank of grayish mud stretch-
ing out into the lake, and Hodge offered to go after them.
That venture was very nearly the death of him. He ran
out onto the bank but had gone only a yard or two when
he started to sink in the ooze.

"Quicksand," he shouted, and turned about. But the
action of turning made him sink deeper, and his legs were
in a moment buried to the knees. His efforts to lift one up
thrust the other down. He was sinking to a horrible death
before my eyes. I could not get to him without getting into
the jelly-like stuff myself. I went out on the mud as far as
I dared, and in trying to reach me, Hodge fell forward.
I thought him gone then, but his falling forward was the
saving of him. Immediately he ceased to sink so fast, and

reaching out with the musket, I slowly helped him to safety. I don't suppose he had been more than five minutes at the most on the quicksand, but between fright and effort he was thoroughly exhausted and lay on his back, breathing deeply, his face pale as ashes and the sweat pouring from him.

"I was within an inch of dying," he said. He lay resting, breathing very heavily, for some time and then groped around among the reeds and grasses for something to get the mud off his clothes. He needed a great quantity of grass for this task, and in groping he found something reddish and flat which I thought to be a piece of bark from a tree but which proved to be part of the blade of a seaman's cutlass, broken off about six inches from the point.

"What do you make of that?" he asked, throwing it to me.

I didn't know what to make of it. I felt the edge of it with my thumb and was surprised that, despite the rust, it retained a degree of sharpness. I cleaned it on my boot and found that without any great degree of effort the rust could be removed to show the gleaming steel below.

"This was broken recently," I said. "Certainly since Silver has been on this island."

Hodge looked thoughtfully at the broken end of the cutlass and then at the quicksand in which he had almost lost his life. "There's a fortunate man for you—that Silver," he said slowly. "Providence kept a weather eye open for him and no mistake. Here's all his shipmates lost and him alone saved. And here he is wrecked not on any ordinary island but one that's stiff with treasure. And here's this quicksand that he might have plunged into the same as I did. And yet he missed it. And then here's the first ship that calls at this island is a merchant vessel out of Salem when you'd think that Flint's crew would have been here as fierce as starving rats in a butcher's shambles. Ah, he's a lucky man, that Silver. No doubt about it. The first bit of bad luck he had was to break his cutlass hereabouts—cutting grass, do you suppose?"

"What do you mean by that?" I asked.

"It's my opinion that Silver wasn't alone when he got here. There was others with him, and the last drop of life that one of them had went when his cutlass broke on this very spot. He's a powerful man, is Long John, shoulders on him like a bull. One-legged or not, I wouldn't like to cross Silver, and him with a cutlass in that big fist of his."

The bosun's words hit me between wind and water, as the saying goes, and a score of terrible possibilities crowded into my mind. I recalled the death of Mr. Arrow on our second day on the island, explained as an accident and yet a very strange accident to happen to such a man. I recalled Green reporting the smell of wood smoke in the air during our first night in Captain Kidd's Anchorage. And then there was Long John going off each day to get fruit, and always insisting that, although one-legged, he did not need help. Was he really just gathering food? Then there was the wall of silver ingots in the back of the cave, and the four heavy chests of gems. Surely Flint would have buried his treasure, not left it in a cave for any chance castaway to find. If Flint had buried it, who had dug it up and brought it to the cave?

"Hodge," I said, "do you suppose there are others ashore besides Silver?"

Hodge, for answer, threw the cutlass point to me. "Tom," he said, "that there blade was broke less than six months ago and broke in a fight and Silver wasn't fighting with himself. I think there's more ashore than Silver and I think they are maybe lying low until we get all that treasure aboard. The last of the treasure went aboard this morning. The brig's watered, provisioned, and armed. Part of the crew—most of the crew—is ashore, like us. If there's more men ashore, Flint's hands, let's say, and Long John leading them, there isn't a better time to seize the *Jane* than now."

"Come," I cried, "there isn't a moment to lose. We must get back to the brig immediately."

Our shortest route to the inlet where the *Jane* lay was due north, with the swamp on our right-hand side. A good landmark would have been the hill on the northern side of the inlet in which the treasure cave was, but that was not to be seen through the forest of evergreen oaks which we now had to make our way through. The branches of these trees spread close to the ground like giant fans and were festooned with Spanish moss. The ground was thick with mold into which we sank at every step, and clouds of mosquitoes lived under these trees and feasted on us as we struggled along. We had soon thrown away the ducks and

92.

we would have thrown away some of our clothing but for the mosquitoes, which were able to bite even through the stuff of our shirts. They battened on our bare arms, faces, and necks, so that we were covered with welts from all their stings.

Eventually we came to a small escarpment or cliff, not much more than breast-high, and when we had climbed this and plunged on perhaps three hundred yards, the mosquitoes suddenly left us. We were not now among oaks but among pines and could feel a little stirring of a sea breeze, which after the heavy air of that moss-hung forest was like the renewal of life itself. Here, despite our urgency, we had to rest for a moment. My arms showed a dozen little trickles of blood from the bites of the mosquitoes and my left arm was beginning to swell to twice its size. We flung ourselves on the ground, panting, and then heard from ahead the report of a musket, followed by two or three more.

"Come on," I yelled, and plunged forward. We had, I suppose, half a mile yet to go to get to the south side of the bay, so it was twenty minutes before, bursting through the last of the trees, we saw the calm waters of North Inlet before us. There the *Jane* lay, utterly peaceful, scarcely stirring at her anchor. The brig's yawl swung alongside and she was exactly as I had last seen her, except for one terrible change.

The British ensign had been taken down from the staff on her stern and in its place now hung the skull and cross-

bones—the dreaded flag of piracy. From the brig came a
snatch of song sung in a thin, quavering tenor. The words
reached us clearly across the bay:

> Fifteen men on a Dead Man's Chest—
> Yo-ho-ho, and a bottle of rum!
> Drink and the devil had done for the rest—
> Yo-ho-ho, and a bottle of rum!

THE SHOCK OF so terrible a turnabout—to lose ship and treasure and face the prospect of being marooned on a desert island for the rest of my days (if indeed I were not killed)—deprived me of all reason for the moment. I could only stare at the *Jane*, struggling to accept the truth of what I saw. It was Hodge who first recovered. He touched me on the shoulder and, stooping, motioned that we should get back out of sight among the trees, and this we did without being seen from the brig.

"What's left of the crew may be up in the cave," I said. "We should join them. Perhaps the brig can be retaken."

Hodge shook his head. "Better lie low for a while until we find out what has happened," he said. "We can go up to the cave, and should. But lie low, mate—that's the ticket.

If they're all prisoners up there, we don't want to join them."

This was eminently sensible advice, and so, with one last glance at the *Jane*, we withdrew into the pine woods and started making our way around the end of North Inlet to the treasure cave. It was dark by the time we got there, for we were delayed finding a place to cross the sluggish river that debouched into the North Inlet, and with our recent experience of quicksands were not inclined to take risks. Twilight in these regions lasted but half an hour and then all was pitch-black under the trees, with fireflies here and there exploding into dashes of greenish light.

The cave had a kind of natural protection in the front in the palmettos with their thorns which grew out, but we managed to avoid the worst of these by coming in obliquely from the southwest, where we also had the cover of a spur of the hill to conceal us until we were almost at the cave mouth. Night, then, was well established when we were within a hundred yards of the entrance and could see the glimmer and flicker of a fire from within. We could hear heavy breathing, punctuated by an occasional grunt and low moaning. Hodge sniffed the air and whispered in my ear the one word "Rum," and almost immediately I caught the rich, fruity aroma of it.

Keeping close to the shadows, we stole to the mouth of the cave, and since the firelight illuminated but a small area, we were able to see only a portion of the interior. Smigley and Green lay propped against the side of the cave, their

96.

hands tied behind them. Smigley had a rough bandage on his head through which a dark stain showed. Sweeney, the sailmaker, lay dead just outside the cave, and there were several men beyond, all tied up, hand and foot. On guard at the entrance were two figures in tattered clothing whose straggling long hair and beards gave them the appearance of wild animals rather than human beings. They had each a bare cutlass across his knees and a brace of pistols in his waistband. One, directly facing me, had a livid cutlass scar clean across his nose to the turn of his jaw—a terrible wound that had divided his face diagonally and in healing had left the two portions slightly out of line with each other.

"I'd say Kingston or Vera Cruz," said this one. "But it's all the same to me, so's I get my lay. Whatever Long John says, that will be it, and I don't reckon there's any one fool enough to cross his hawse."

"That's a man with a head on him, that Silver," said the other. "If they'd listened to Long John at the start, and laid off the rum, we'd never have struck and we'd have been out of here eighteen months ago. But rum they must have, and Jacobs, he weren't the man to say no when they'd tapped the barrel."

The other thrust with his boot at the end of a log, and a sheet of flames and sparks rose suddenly into the night, making me withdraw quickly into the shadows, lest I be seen. "That's what comes of crew's elections," he said. "I seen sheep had more sense than seamen. Gentlemen of fortune, is it? Well, they'll muck right in when the rum's running, and never think of anything but what's before them."

"Well," said the other, "right of election is part of the articles. And if a crew votes for grog, grog they have a right to have. T' aint for hard work and hazing they put to sea, but to live free and take their pleasure, dooty done."

"Dooty done," snorted the other. "Running up on a reef on a dark night, three sheets to the wind, ain't my idea of dooty done, nor yours either, if you'd use your head. As for articles, Flint wasn't one to abide by them—nor Billie Bones either. And we've learned a thing or two about articles from Long John since we've all been ashore here so cozy waiting for another ship. Fourteen of us there was as made shore when the old *Walrus* struck, and there's seven of us left. And you know what happened to the rest. Don't go ajawing about articles and deputations to Long John."

"Not I," said the first. "If Long John was to decide to put in with that treasure at the royal dock at Spithead, I'd trim sheets handsome for him. I still get the horrors thinking of Marrow's end."

"Marrow was a fool," said the other. "And a man don't last long in quicksand, anyway."

That settled both the mystery of the broken cutlass and of how Long John and these rogues had come to be wrecked. They'd voted for rum, and Jacobs, whom I took to be their captain, hadn't been man enough to oppose them. With the lookouts drunk or partly drunk, they had run up on a reef. That refrain which we had heard from aboard the *Jane* echoed in my mind:

> Fifteen men on a Dead Man's Chest—
> Yo-ho-ho, and a bottle of rum!
> Drink and the devil had done for the rest—
> Yo-ho-ho, and a bottle of rum!

Someone groaned from inside the cave and called for water and was answered by an oath and a threat. But the other guard got up and, picking up a pannikin, went into the depths of the cave. He was back almost immediately and, seating himself by the fire again, said, "Silver said to treat them gentle. He's a need of hands, and two wrecks on one voyage wouldn't be to his liking."

"Left to me, I'd cut the throat of that captain, and the rest would volunteer quick enough," said the first guard.

"That was never Silver's way," was the reply. "He's a coaxing man, is Silver until aroused, and he'll have half of them eating out of his hand this time tomorrow night, mark my words."

They fell then to talking of other matters—their whack, as they called it, of the treasure, and to what port they were likely to sail with it. We had learned, however, that there were only seven of them—eight, including Silver. That was enough to handle the brig, given fair weather. But fair weather was not to be expected, with ahead that same threat of hurricanes which had persuaded Captain Samuels to put in at the island for topmasts. So Silver would try to persuade at least some of the *Jane*'s crew to join him.

Again it seemed that there were only two ashore, since one had had to leave for a moment to answer the call for water. Given the benefit of surprise and a little luck, Hodge and I might be able to overcome the two of them. But a musket shot would rouse those on the ship, and we had no surety that the arms our men had brought with them had not been gathered up and taken back on board the brig. If we were to overpower the guards, it must be without a shot being fired. So we withdrew some distance and debated the problem. We would never have such an opportunity of liberating the crew again, so we must not fail.

In the end we hit upon a plan which, though desperate, was entirely simple. One of us would distract the attention of both guards, while the other stole into the cave and liberated at least some of the crew. The first one was to allow himself to be taken and brought captive into the cave, when the freed crew would overpower the captors. Hodge volunteered to provide the distraction, though there was a very considerable danger that he might be shot. He stole off into the darkness and came blundering through the palmettos from some distance away, calling out for Captain Samuels. The two guards turned immediately and jumped to their feet, their pistols in their hands, and moved away from the fire toward him. As soon as they left the entrance to the cave, I slipped inside, keeping to the shadows, my sheath knife ready.

The first man I found was Mr. Hogan, our quiet, even-tempered sailing master. I cut him free, whispering in his ear at the same time to say nothing but find what arms he could. He in return whispered that Captain Samuels lay bound opposite him. I felt blood on the captain's clothes as I cut the ropes binding his arms, but whatever his hurt, he asked me only if I had not an extra knife. I gave him Hodge's, for knowing that Hodge would be taken, we had seen no sense in his keeping it. I had just time to give the musket to Becker, the ox of a coxun, with a warning not to fire lest he rouse the ship, when the two pirates reappeared, thrusting Hodge before them.

"He's done for," Hodge was saying. "He was lost in the quicksand. I nearly died trying to save him. Look at the mud on me. But what's happened here? Where's Captain Samuels?"

"You'll find out soon enough," said one of the guards with a chuckle. They entered the cave, one carrying a lantern and going ahead and the other following, thrusting Hodge, his hands already tied, before him. They passed Becker and against the glow of the fire I saw the big coxun rise slowly, clubbing the musket I had given him. He and Sweeney, whose body lay stiff in death only a few feet from him, had been close friends. He swung the musket silently and the blow he dealt the man with Hodge would have felled a dray horse. Down he went like a dropped sack, and the other guard, whirling around with an oath, was seized by Captain Samuels. He cried out, dropped the lantern, gave a kind of sigh, and himself fell to the ground. All was over in a matter of seconds. The lantern rolled away, the flame turning first orange and then blue, and I

101.

snatched it up before it went out. The man lay stretched face down on the floor, Hodge's knife driven to the hilt into his heart by the captain. He was quite dead.

Captain Samuels examined him, unmoved, in the flickering light of the candle lantern, and said, "I'd give my share of the treasure and a year's pay on top of it if that man had been Long John Silver."

12

CAPTAIN SAMUELS WAS FOR attempting to retake the *Jane* immediately. He was boiling with wrath that his ship had been taken from him, and by pirates, and of all pirates, by Silver. Silver had duped him as readily as a child, despite the captain's distrust of the man. The tale of that duplicity, which I learned later, is soon told. When all the treasure was aboard, and Captain Samuels and one or two others with it, Silver had got the greater part of the crew into the cave and produced a cask of rum, which he said he had put by for just that occasion.

It is not hard to persuade seamen, once ashore, to take a drink, and it must be acknowledged that few crews had such a cause for celebration, as they thought, as ours. First one had taken a drink, and then another, and before long the crew had utterly lost all guard and discipline and determined on finishing the cask before going on board. Peasbody, the officer in charge, should have prevented all this, but Peasbody had no real authority with the men and, indeed, hoping to show himself just such a fellow as they, had joined them in a toast. After that, it was no trouble to persuade him to one more, and he had soon lost all competence as an officer. He remembered enough of his duty, however, to get back to the ship and report that the hands were all drunk ashore. Captain Samuels left immediately, taking Hogan, the sailing master, with him, and leaving Peasbody aboard protesting childishly that he had done his best to keep discipline among the men.

It was not until the captain was inside the cave and haranguing the crew that Silver summoned his rogues, whom he had visited each day hidden about the island. There was a sharp tussle, some of the men not being entirely gone in drink, but men stupefied with rum and taken by surprise were no match for the remnant of Flint's crew. Captain Samuels went down, felled by a blow from Long John's crutch, and Sweeney had been shot dead, and four others gravely wounded. The crew, in short, were soon subdued and tied up, and then it had been an easy matter for Silver to take the brig, defended as it was only by Peasbody and two hands, who could only gape as the pirates came alongside. One did try to get to the swivel in the ship's waist, we learned later, but it was a futile gesture. It took three hands to serve that piece, and all he got for his pains was a blow on the side of the head with the flat of a cutlass.

104.

Released then by Hodge and me, Captain Samuels was determined to launch a counterattack immediately, and it was the sailing master, Mr. Hogan, who pointed out to him, patiently but firmly, that this might lead only to the slaughter of his unarmed crew.

"We're seventeen," said Captain Samuels, "and they are but six, including Silver. Don't talk to me of slaughter."

"We are thirteen, sir, not counting the heavily wounded, and have but a single musket, two pistols, and two cutlasses among us," said the sailing master. "Once the firearms are discharged in an assault, it will be unarmed men against six fully armed desperadoes, every one of them a veteran of a score of boardings."

That made Captain Samuels hesitate. However many men he had, there was no gainsaying that our hands were green when it came to fighting. To pit inexperienced, unarmed men against Flint's hands, fully armed, was scarcely a plan for victory.

"If you have another scheme," said Captain Samuels, "speak up. We have but a few hours of dark and we must make the best use of them. I'll listen to anything any man has to say, for we are all together in this. We must either retake the brig or face spending the rest of our lives on this island, if we are not cut down like so much pork first. That's the choice, a desperate choice calling for desperate measures."

"And all the treasure gone," muttered Green. Captain Samuels looked at him sharply but refrained from saying a word.

"The ebbs set in soon, I think," said Smigley. "We could run her aground."

"And what good would that do?" demanded the captain.

"Well, sir," said Smigley in his plodding way, "if we had the boats and we cut her cable, the ebb would take her out to the entrance of the inlet and she would run aground likely on that point there. And they couldn't refloat her, for they could not get an anchor out to kedge off, using the windlass, and they couldn't take a line ashore without swimming with it, and we own the shore. They got the brig, but we got the island."

"She'd float off when the tide turned," said the captain. "Or they could lighten her and refloat her without waiting for the tide."

"Not while we got a musket and shot," said Smigley. "For as soon as a man comes on deck, he could be picked off. They wouldn't dare show themselves."

"Who is the best hand with a musket?" asked the captain.

"Becker," said Mr. Hogan. "I've seen him put out a candle at a hundred yards, and that with a horse pistol."

Captain Samuels hesitated. The temptation with so many men at his back to rush the ship and retake it was all but overwhelming. He had darkness and surprise in his favor, and such an attack would certainly succeed had we plenty of arms.

But the lack of arms, and the certainty that, should the assault fail, then all was lost, lent him caution. Hodge, the bosun, pointed out that, while we might command the deck in daylight with a musket ashore, there was nothing we could do in the dark. "They have only to wait for the night flood and there is nothing we could do to stop them refloating the ship," he said, and this was entirely true.

In the end, a combination of the two plans was agreed on. We would cut the *Jane*'s cable first and then rush the ship. If we succeeded in retaking her, it would be easy for us to refloat her. If we failed, there was still the prospect that the ship would go aground and Silver would be unable to leave with her, at least immediately.

This agreed, Captain Samuels sorted out the men, leaving the four heavily wounded in the cave to await the outcome. This still gave us odds of two to one. The arms were divided out, and those who had nothing searched about for anything that might be useful. By the time we reached the bottom of the cliff, we were all armed after a fashion, though some had only a large cobble slung in a neckerchief for a weapon.

One of the boats—the small gig—had been left ashore for the use of the two guards at the cave. This could take only five men at best, and even so, she would be loaded to the gunwales and in danger of swamping. The yawl we presumed was tied alongside the brig, but though we could see the brig's yards and masts against the starlit sky, her hull was in darkness and we could not be sure of the whereabouts of the yawl. While we were debating whether to go out for the yawl with the gig or have someone swim for her, Mr. Hogan pointed to a faint luminescence, which threw the outline of a hill to the east of the bay into silhouette.

107.

"Moonrise," he whispered. "In fifteen minutes—ten—the attempt will be impossible."

That settled the matter. Those who had the arms went into the gig. The rest waded in to swim, everybody keeping to the west of the *Jane*, so as to remain as long as possible in her shadow and out of the moonlight. Hodge had muffled the oars as soon as we got the gig, and taken the additional precaution of wetting the tholes thoroughly to reduce any sound. The captain, Mr. Hogan, Hodge, Becker, and I went in the gig, Hodge and I handling the oars, Becker up forward (despite his weight) with his musket ready, and the captain at the tiller in the stern.

My heart was thumping so heavily that I thought all around must hear it as we pushed off. The gig gave a little scrape on the gravel where she touched, and then we were away, gliding toward the *Jane*, rowing with the greatest care, and passing the swimmers, who looked like so many otters in the water around us.

"We must board by the waist," whispered Captain Samuels. "Becker, if you get a clear view of the watch as we come alongside, bring him down."

"He'll have the moon behind him, I fancy," said Becker, and the coolness of his reply did a great deal to steady my nerve.

All went well until we were nearly alongside the *Jane*, and then we met with our first mishap. The ebb had set in, and the brig, swinging on her cable, had turned to interpose her hull between us and the rising moon. We had then plenty of deep shadow for our approach, but in the excitement we forgot about the yawl. When we were a few feet from the brig's side, there was the yawl swinging on her painter clear across our path. Becker saw her suddenly loom out of the dark and reached to fend her off, but she was at the end of her line and so could not be pushed aside. The gig hit her with a thump like a drum and hung up on her, not yet alongside and unable to go farther.

"Who's there?" somebody shouted from the brig, and a figure appeared, leaning over the bulwark amidships. I have never seen a man as cool as Becker. He had the musket up in a moment, took a steady aim, fired, and the man staggered back and collapsed out of sight on the deck.

"Give way," yelled Captain Samuels, and Hodge and I put our backs into the oars, slamming the gig and the yawl into the side of the *Jane*. The gig swamped immediately and the impact knocked Mr. Hogan, who had half risen, right into my lap. But Captain Samuels strode with one bound onto the yawl and was on the deck of the *Jane* in a moment. Somehow we trooped up behind him in time to meet a rush of men coming from the cabin. I discharged my pistol point-blank at a figure charging down on me, but the flint was wet and would not spark. I was bowled over in a moment and would have been dispatched there and then but for the swivel. I had fallen partly under the gun, and the cutlass stroke, aimed at my chest, glanced off the barrel. I still had the pistol and, scrambling up, brought it down on the arm of my attacker and heard a bone crack at the blow.

That one successful blow wonderfully cleared my mind.

I cocked the pistol again, leveled it, and fired, and this time the flint flashed and the pistol discharged with a roar. The light of the discharge seemed to illuminate the whole bay. I caught a glimpse of Captain Samuels wrestling with a man whose head was wrapped in a whitish cloth, and farther off I saw Silver lunge at Becker, who had only a clubbed musket with which to defend himself. Becker was the stronger of the two, but he was no match for Silver's cunning. The sea cook feinted with his cutlass and then, shifting to his good leg, drove the end of his crutch like a ramrod into Becker's chest, and down he went.

Long John didn't give him another look. He turned and was on the point of engaging the captain, who was still struggling with the man with the white kerchief, when the *Jane* grounded with a shock that knocked us all off our feet and set her rigging humming like the strings of a viol. Long John's cutlass was flung, by this accident, right to my hand, and I was up in a moment, while the sea cook floundered to gain his footing. One-legged, unarmed, and minus his crutch, which had also been knocked from him, he was still full of fight. He pulled himself erect with his hands and glared about like a cornered bull, his face pale in the light of the moon, which had now risen, and his fair hair stuck to his forehead by some blow. The rest of the crew had now gained the deck, and the fight was over and the brig ours. Silver realized this in a moment and turned to me.

"Ah, Tom," he said, "looks like me and Mr. Arrow is to be shipmates again." Plainly he thought that I would cut him down unarmed there and then.

"Long John," I said, "it will not be I that sends you to join Mr. Arrow, but the king's judge and the king's jury. You're a pirate and a cutthroat. It was you who killed Mr. Arrow. That I know now. And you'll hang on a Boston gibbet with your crutch about your neck."

The change that came over him in that moment was remarkable. Gone was all the courage and defiance. His face grew pale. He looked desperately around, as if seeking a chance to escape. Poor Becker, scarcely breathing, lay on his back before him, but he had no thought for him or the others, dead and dying, around.

"I'll not swing, Tom," he said in a strange, hoarse voice. "No, by the powers. Not I. Roberts maybe, and Kidd. But not Long John." There was a deal of spirit and determination in what he said. But there was a deal more of fear, which was astonishing in such a man as Silver.

13

WE HAD PAID a heavy price for the recapture of the brig. Poor Becker never recovered. Long John's terrible thrust with his crutch had stove his chest in over his heart and he died that night without regaining consciousness. I had known the man ashore only remotely, and for the short length of our present voyage. He came of a sheep-raising family beyond Salem, but when I learned that he was dead, I burst into tears, all the tensions and dangers of our voyage overwhelming me and demanding release. There was no consoling me. I think I wept not only for Becker but for all the horrors and cruelties of the world symbolized in that terrible island. The others left me alone, Captain Samuels saying to Mr. Hogan, who tried to comfort me, "Let him be. He'll be a man when he is done." Indeed, when at last the tears stopped, I felt very old and very different from the person I had been before.

Mr. Hogan himself had received a cutlass stroke across his chest. Calkins, a plain seaman coming from New York, was in a serious state with a bullet through his knee and his back laid open, again by a cutlass, when he went down, and Scatterfield, another of our crew, lay dead by the foot of the mizzen, almost decapitated.

We had lost, then, two dead, two seriously hurt, and several others with minor hurts—not counting our four wounded in the cave ashore. But Silver's losses were far heavier. His two guards ashore were dead, Becker had killed the one on duty on the brig, I had dispatched the man who had come at me, and Captain Samuels another, and the two who remained were both wounded, one so badly that it appeared he must lose his arm.

"Well," said Captain Samuels, reckoning the cost of the battle, "there's what comes of treasure. There's seven died by your hand on the island, I'm told, Silver. Add the result of tonight's work and those lost in the wreck of your ship, and you have something over a score gone to their reward, I fancy. That's something to have on your conscience, I would think."

"Well now," said Silver, who had recovered himself to a remarkable degree, "not wishing to offend, and so leaving out your own hands, Captain, most of them others was swabs. There wasn't what you could call a seaman among ten of them. Begging or cutting throats or picking pockets was the best they could do for themselves ashore. You can't lay the wreck of the *Walrus* to my account. I'm a seaman myself, as I think you'll allow, and left to me, there'd have been no rum going until I had that treasure ashore. As for them others, I reckon there's few will miss them, and killing them might be reckoned by some a public service."

The effrontery of the man was beyond belief. Here he was on a ship drenched with blood of his own shedding, as it were, and his conscience not even pricked.

"By thunder," said Captain Samuels, "you're a hard man, John Silver."

"Aye," said Silver coolly. "And lived hard from a boy. I saw my own father dancing against the sky at Tyburn, and my mother in chains in Bedlam. Orphans whose fathers was hanged don't make good deacons, and you can lay to that." And he spat defiantly on the deck.

The wounded were all attended to by the captain, who, I think from the very vigor of his attack, had escaped hurt himself, though he had a scalp wound from that previous blow given to him by Silver. He proved deft with a sail needle, sewing up cuts, and kept a brandy bottle handy for those whose pain, under his rough surgery, would be beyond bearing. The pirate with the smashed hand had the innocent name of Dick and begged that as much as possible should be spared.

"Why?" demanded the captain, passing him the brandy bottle. "You'll have little enough use for it with a rope around your neck." The look on the fellow's face tore my heart. To kill a man in battle was one thing. But to hold over him, alive, the threat of execution, was beyond me, though Captain Samuels took a grim delight in the prospect that Silver and his two remaining men would certainly hang. Indeed, he assured them, treating their wounds, that he was but saving them for the gallows.

The dead we buried ashore the next day—Becker and Scatterfield and Sweeney and Haskins in graves side by side, and the pirate dead some distance apart. I thought, as the captain read the funeral service from the Book of Common Prayer, of those other graves at the south end of the island inside the stockade—Redruth and Mr. Arrow, and nearby that of Flint's bosun, Job Anderson—and I was filled with such a horror of the island on which so many had died that I wished with all my heart to be a thousand leagues away from it and never to have to look on any part of it again. Nor was I alone in these sentiments, for as soon as the funeral was over, Mr. Hogan approached the captain with a petition from the heavily wounded men who were still in the cave, begging that they should not be left behind when we sailed. The captain was strongly opposed to taking them with us.

"There's two, maybe three of them, will die aboard that might well live ashore," he said. "I'll pledge my word to send a ship for them from the first port I touch, or the first ship I speak at sea."

"Sir," said Mr. Hogan, "they'd sooner take their chances on board. That island is a kind of cemetery in their minds. Viewing it as they do, they would not live on that island any longer than they would live on the brig. Of that I am sure."

Captain Samuels was still opposed to taking them. Apart from endangering their lives, there was the matter of endangering his ship. He had lost, between death and wounds, nine men, leaving but a handful to handle the brig in the heavy weather ahead. No hands could he spare to tend wounded men. And yet the well hands insisted that the wounded should not be left in that terrible place.

So all were brought on board, two having to be lowered on a whip down the cliff. A hospital of sorts was made in the forecastle—the bulkheads being padded with what sails could be spared, to ease them in bumping against the ship's sides, and the worst of them being put in the companionway cabins aft in hammocks.

When this was done, the ship's boats were brought aboard and the sound hands manned the capstan forward to bring up the anchor. I went to the cathead with a bowline to fish the anchor to the side when it came clear, and my last glimpse of North Inlet was of those two skeletons lying on the bottom, one with its head in the other's lap. A little touch of wind coming down Foremast Hill filled the topsails. In half an hour we had cleared the inlet, and in two hours only the tip of Spyglass showed on the horizon to the east, and this was soon lost in clouds. That massive peak was our last as well as our first glimpse of Flint's Island.

We sailed westward toward a flaming sunset in a ship full of treasure and, I might say also, full of blood.

14

CAPTAIN SAMUELS'S INTENTION NOW was to return, avoiding the uncertain ports of the Spanish or French, and when we were well clear of Flint's Island we set our course north, intending to steer this track until we had run down our latitude, and then we had only to turn due west to reach the Georgia coast, clear of the uncertain Floridas. The colony of Georgia, with Savannah as its principal port, was the first place where we could expect succor in our stricken condition. A northward course would take us wide both of Hispaniola, which besides being in the dominion of the King of Spain was a notorious haunt of pirates, and also of the Bahama Islands, on whose coral so many fine ships have been lost.

Had we a full crew, Silver would have been confined

to irons during the voyage. But we were desperately short of hands, with wounded to be attended to, and putting Silver in irons would make one more useless hand who had to be fed. Captain Samuels consulted with Mr. Hogan, Peasbody, and myself, and, very much against his conviction, was persuaded to leave Silver free so he could cook for us, relieving a man for ship handling.

That decision, thrust upon him, cost the captain sorely, but there was no avoiding it. He complained more than once that every spoonful of food nearly choked him, and, served with soup, pronounced it "devil's broth."

Silver did more than the cooking. Taking the meals to them, he found time to tend to the wounded men, whom he treated with patience and kindness. Despite the fate in store for him, he spread a degree of cheerfulness among the men in the forecastle which was wonderful to see. Whatever wanted to be done, Silver was there to do it, and his very presence was as good as medicine for the wounded hands.

Calkins, whose shattered knee made amputation seem inevitable, was cheered by Silver's saying that he had not missed his own leg after a month or so and in some ways found it an advantage to be without it. "I can stand on this timber of mine all day and feel as rested as if I was sitting down yarning," he asserted.

Another, who feared to die and begged for a Bible, Silver assured had no need for a chaplain yet. "You're as stout as a nine-inch plank," he said. "A week or two and you'll be begging for a trick at the wheel."

And so he went about, and between his cheer and his food

the men seemed to forget that he, and he alone, was the source of all their miseries. The well hands at first avoided him, but he was not the man to be set down by a rebuff, and they began after a while to admire his spirit. Indeed, were it possible to discount his black past, I would certainly say that Silver was twice the man of anyone else aboard, Captain Samuels alone excepted. Some, however, were not deceived. Hodge said plainly that he would as soon have a serpent aboard as Long John, and Captain Samuels, of course, would never say a word directly to him or spare him as much as a look. Still, by the time we had reached the latitude of the Bahamas, though many miles to the east of them, Silver had to a great degree gained favor with many of the crew and spread a cheer which was hard to resist.

He had his solemn moments, though, and once, finding me alone, begged me most earnestly to take care of his parrot, should he be condemned. "That bird's the only friend I have in this world," he said. " 'Twould make it easier if I knew he was in good hands when I'm gone." It was scarcely credible that a man who had cut down seven of his companions on that island, and I do not know how many in a life devoted to wickedness, should be concerned about the fate of a parrot, but there was no mistaking the earnestness of his plea. I suppose that the affection, trust, and companionship which Silver, from the days of his childhood, had been unable to find in his fellow man, he found in that wicked bird.

On another occasion, coming on deck a little before dawn, he asked me very solemnly whether I thought that prayer would be of any avail to a man in his position. I told him that God turned quickly to the Prodigal and the angels themselves rejoiced at the repentance of a sinner.

"Well now," he said thoughtfully, "I wouldn't look for cheering on coming into port—no, not I. Just to slip in in a dying wind in the dark would be all I could hope for—and more than I have call to look for, says you."

You will recall that when we had cut her cable in North Inlet, the *Jane* had run aground, and although at the time no damage was observed, we now found that she had a slow leak, which could be kept under control by ten minutes at the pump at the start of each watch. We would have had no great concern over this, but for a menacing change of the weather in the latitude of the Bahamas.

The wind fell very light for a day and a night and there followed two days when the sky was coated with a layer of cloud as if washed with dirty milk. In the second dogwatch of the third day, a slow swell set in from the southeast, and darker clouds, like wisps of cobweb, appeared, flying westwards. There was wind overhead then, but at the surface of the sea not enough air stirred to fill our sails, and our yards clashed in their slings, and the canvas flapped, as we rolled on the uneasy sea, with a report like thunder. We well knew what lay in store, and all hands were sent aloft to stow down canvas. Long John, after studying the sky and the rolling seas, went below without a word. Lifelines were rigged about the deck, extra doggings put on the hatches, and weather cloths rigged about the wheel to protect the helmsman.

The gale came with the dark on that third day. There was no sunset—just the disappearance of light, while south and east of us a black bar of cloud, solid as iron, formed and moved toward us. No ship, whatever the experience of her captain, was ever ready for that force of wind. Before the wind hit, we heard in the darkness the roaring and thundering of the seas around. Then the wind struck, leaping on us out of the dark, and flung the *Jane* leaning over on her beam ends. She lay there as if she must capsize. Slowly she righted herself and had hardly staggered up when the first of those terrible seas we had heard thundering to weather crashed into her stern and the whole hull was lost in a roaring cataract. I was swept off my feet and down into the storm of water which covered the waist of the ship. There I would certainly have gone overboard, but I was brought by chance up against the foremast life rail and, gripping the halyards in my arms, held on for life.

It was minutes before the brig could struggle free of the grip of the sea and I could get to safety at the break of the deck. The yawl, stowed amidships, had come off her chocks and was in danger of being smashed to pieces. She could be cut free to join the gig, which was already overboard, and that was my intent, but Captain Samuels signaled she was to be relashed. How we managed this, I do not know. Twice we had her almost cinched down and twice were washed off our feet by seas boarding us. In the end we made her fast, the carpenter driving enough wedges under her, as he said later, to build another boat.

I had thought the first hour of the storm might see us

through the worst of it, but the winds mounted hour by hour, and in heavy gusts a man caught on deck would have been blown overboard but for the lifelines.

About midnight a terrible moon showed, white as death in a sky that seemed to be of polished black metal. The sea around us, in the ghastly moonlight, was like a snowfield, being all foam and showing only here and there the writhing darkness of the water. Over this stark ocean, when dawn came, tiny birds fluttered on trembling wings—Mother Carey's chickens, for whom a full gale is fair weather.

The shrieking of the wind in our rigging was past all description, and added to this was the terrible roaring of the water, as sea after sea rushed down upon us seeking to destroy us. By dawn we had endured ten hours of this fury, the wind increasing all the time but moving ever to the southwest. About noon there was a little lessening of the wind, and clinging to the lifelines, we were able to rig the pump. We discovered that whatever damage had been done to the hull in the grounding at North Inlet was very much worse now. Four hours of pumping were needed before we sucked air. Thereafter, the pump was manned whenever the opportunity offered, but for the next two days, during which the storm moved around to southeast and then passed away, we could do nothing but work to save rather than sail the brig.

On the first day of the storm, we had only ship's biscuit and cold pork for food. But in the forenoon watch of the second day, Long John appeared on deck through the companionway aft, struggling on his crutch but still able to

122.

carry in one hand a pot of hot soup with a pannikin in it. He had an old sea cloak lashed over him to protect the kettle of soup as much as himself, and was as cheerful as a schoolboy on a holiday.

"How did you contrive this?" I cried.

"I have a trick or two," roared Long John in my ear, "and keep a little firewood in my bunk with me." I could not but admire him. Pirate he certainly was, and murderous too. But he was a seaman to put beside Drake.

Captain Samuels stared at the steaming soup and turned away. But when Long John had gone, I persuaded him to have a pannikin of it, it being his duty to keep up his strength, and he did so, swallowing it as if it were poison. But I think he too was impressed, though he uttered not a syllable of thanks.

On the fourth day, then, the storm had diminished suffi-ciently to set reefed topgallants and an outer jib, and we were able to assess our hurts. "Ship first and then the crew" was ever Captain Samuels's way, and indeed so the sea de-mands, so I was soon down with Smigley in the forehold, looking for our leak. We found three ribs cracked above the futtocks, and two planks stove in such a way that there was no repairing them from within the hull. The ribs we sistered—that is, fastened supporting pieces beside them—but the planks were stove right beside the ribs, and though patching reduced the leak, we could not make a sound job of it. In the end, we resorted to fothering as well. That is to say, put an old sail over the side, folded, and half a gallon of paint dumped in the fold. This, positioned over the stove

123.

planks, was driven by water pressure into the break. Smigley went over the side in a bosun's chair with a pouch full of nails to tack the sail in place as well as he could above the water, but we had to rely on lines passed beneath the hull to secure it, and these, our bottom being foul, were likely to chafe through on barnacles. Although this patching and fothering did not entirely stop the leak, it greatly reduced the amount of water we were taking.

"Fair-weather patching," grumbled Smigley when he came on board again. "We can't fetch Savannah with old sails for planking."

The old carpenter always took such a gloomy view of every circumstance that I paid no attention to this remark, but later, during my watch that evening, I was surprised by Hodge's asking whether he might not now alter course to westward to put in perhaps at the Bahamas or, if too far north, the Floridas. I told him I considered that very unlikely —Captain Samuels, in view of the treasure and the uncertainty of our relations with Spain, being determined to make Georgia. That this was so was soon confirmed, for the sky clearing by midafternoon to windward, we shook out the reef in our topgallants and added reefed topsails, and another jib.

"Keep her north," said the captain to the man at the wheel, and the hands belaying the topsail sheets exchanged looks and went forward somewhat sullenly.

15

CALKINS DID NOT survive the storm. In addition to
his smashed knee, he had sustained, you will recall, a cutlass
stroke across the back which had laid the flesh open almost
to the ribs. He had been brought aft to lie in a hammock in
one of the companionway cabins, and in the gale the hammock had had to be lashed to prevent him smashing into the
bulkheads. Nonetheless, the stitches in his back had torn
open, he had lost a deal of blood, and so he died—the fifth
among us to die in the three short weeks since we had
sighted Flint's Island.

Captain Samuels conducted the funeral service, and Calkins's poor belongings, in a battered wooden locker, were
brought aft from the forecastle to be put in the captain's
care. The contrast between the simple honest chest of the

seaman, with its rope handles and his name burned into the top with a hot iron, and those four iron-bound treasure chests alongside of which it was now stowed struck me like a blow. Calkins's contained some sea clothes, foul-weather gear, a suit of brown homespun for going ashore, two pounds of twist tobacco wrapped in sailcloth, some letters (all printed by hand) from his wife, and a sheath knife. The sum of one man's possessions after a life honestly spent did not equal in money the value of the smallest bauble in the treasure chests. The contrast was not lost on Captain Samuels either.

"I'd sooner stand before my Maker with Calkins's chest than all those other four," he said. "There is another world where many of the values held in this one are reversed, and that must be our consolation."

"He'd a wife and a young sister living with him, half-witted," said one of the hands who had brought the chest aft. "And it's in this world that the two of them will have to fend for themselves alone."

"They shall have his full share, to the last farthing," said Captain Samuels. "I will stake my honor on that."

Two others of our crew were now in a bad way, one of them Mr. Hogan, who had fallen into a fever from his wound, and another a man whose seemingly superficial hurt —the result of a pistol ball which had grazed his shoulder —was now swollen and of a greenish tinge with the undeniable stench of gangrene.

Our position, according to the noon sight (our first for five days), put us in the latitude of Florida, though how far east of that coast was a matter of guesswork. Captain Samuels reckoned a hundred leagues, for we had been driven eastward during the gale. Given fair weather, we could make the Florida coast in but three days at the most, and there was now a strong sentiment among the crew for putting in at Florida, whatever might be the disposition of the Spanish.

Silver never said a word one way or the other, though Florida would certainly suit him. He bustled around in the forecastle attending to the wounded, cooking the meals, and handing out a tidbit at the end of the watch to the hands going below. Any destination was better for him than one of the British colonies, and he would not be concerned that the Floridas were Spanish territory. Spanish governors were by no means averse to piracy. Yet I could not say on any direct evidence that Silver was responsible for the crew's growing desire to put in at St. Augustine or some other Florida port.

The matter came to a head before the end of the week. A deputation led by Green called on the captain very politely with a request that he put in at Florida or the nearest land, "to save those in danger of death among us." That wording, I will swear, was Silver's, though he took no part in the deputation, staying close to his galley and his pots.

Captain Samuels dealt with the deputation briefly. He had no charts aboard of the Florida coast, which they all knew to be strewn with reefs. It was Spanish territory and their status once they gained shore would be uncertain.

The Florida coast was feverish, as they well knew, infested with flies, and the sick would be no better off on shore than they would be aboard the brig. Finally, whether we were at war with Spain or not, the Spanish would not part with a brig loaded with treasure which in all probability had been theirs in the first place.

"Bear this in mind," the captain added, "I offered to leave the wounded men ashore on Flint's Island, and they begged to be taken aboard, agreeing to assume any risk. Well, aboard they are and will stay aboard until we fetch the king's domains. The safety of this ship, of the treasure, and every man on her is in my care, and my judgment is that we must avoid foreign ports. You can best serve your own interests by working cheerfully with me until we are off Savannah, which I judge will be the case in a week at most."

Despite the civility with which he received the deputation, there was no disguising the fact that Captain Samuels suspected that Silver lay behind it, and he all the more bitterly regretted the circumstances which had forced him to allow Silver the freedom of the ship. He could, of course, clap him in irons even now. I have no doubt that he weighed doing so. But, outwardly at least, Silver had been a model of good behavior since we left Flint's Island, and to chain him on mere suspicion seemed outrageous and certainly would not set well with the men, among whom Silver was again a favorite.

All went well for a day or so, during which time we made but little northing, the wind being contrary. One evening, having the night watch from eight to midnight of land time, I had stopped in to see poor Mr. Hogan, now confined to his bunk by his wound and a fever. He was awake and we fell to talking about our poor progress and of the disposition of the crew and the plight of the ship.

"Tom," he said, "watch Silver closely. Whatever his present attitude, that man is not to be trusted. If there is trouble, Silver will be behind it. Of that I am sure."

"Have you heard anything?" I asked.

"No," said Hogan. "But has it occurred to you that if Silver could master fourteen of Flint's hands when they were marooned on that island, though he had to kill seven of them, handling this crew will be no great problem for him? Why, I think if the ship's officers were removed, the crew would vote Silver captain tomorrow."

"There's some not deceived by him," I said. "Hodge, for one. And Smigley. And Captain Samuels has his measure to the inch."

"And you?" asked Mr. Hogan.

"I feel sorry for him at times," I said. "Had he had some other kind of childhood, he might have been a man of great parts. It is no easy thing as a boy to see your father hung at Tyburn."

"Tom," said Mr. Hogan. "I no more believe that Silver's father was hung at Tyburn than I believe that Silver lost his leg at Quiberon Bay under Hawke. You see how it is, Tom. If you, with your learning, have some sympathy for him, judge how matters stand with the crew. That's the danger of the man. He is as subtle as a serpent."

He was silent for a moment, and then said, seemingly changing the topic, "Stennis is to lose his arm, I hear."

Stennis was the man whose wound had turned gangrenous. "So it would appear," I said.

"It was Silver who dressed his wound," said Mr. Hogan mildly. "It was Silver, too, who found Calkins bleeding in his hammock and his stitches torn open. I won't have that man near me."

Mr. Hogan's meaning was quite clear to me. He suspected Silver of tampering with the wounded men and so driving the ship closer to crisis. And yet the suspicion was almost too horrible to entertain and I remonstrated with Mr. Hogan about it.

"Tom," said Mr. Hogan, "consider not Silver's words but Silver's deeds. How many men has he killed? How has he lived? How much repentance has he shown over those deaths? Then ask yourself whether Silver would not put a little dirt in a man's wounds or pull open a helpless seaman's stitches to save his own neck. Watch him, Tom. He's up to something. And whatever it is, it may cost us our lives."

I had a chance to talk to the captain that very night, for he came on deck at six bells and, on my saying that I wished to speak to him, took me aside to the taffrail, well out of earshot of the helmsman. I told him of my talk with Mr. Hogan and he listened carefully to every word I said. When I was done, he said I had told him nothing new but his hands were tied for the present. "If I forbid Silver to tend the men and their condition worsens, I will be blamed and held inhuman," he said. "If I put Silver in irons, they'd mutiny in an hour. That man has outmaneuvered me on my own ship. I believe he is more master of my crew, or the greater part of them, than I. But until he makes an overt act, I am powerless to move against him. We must hope for a fair wind and keep our eyes open. Four days now should see us off Savannah and an end to our troubles."

Peasbody was to relieve me at the change of the watch, and before turning in, my mind I suppose running on the ship's troubles, I took a lantern and, going forward, went down into the hold to inspect the leak. All was well enough there, for Smigley, despite the pessimism of his nature, was a fine carpenter, and there was only a slow seepage from the stove planks, which the pumps could well take care of. When I returned on deck, however, to go aft to my own quarters, I noticed the hands still working at the pump, discharging more water than seemed possible since the bilges were last pumped. Troubled, a terrible suspicion flashed through my mind and I scooped up a handful of the water gushing out of the pump and tasted it. It tasted sweet— only slightly brackish.

"What's the matter?" asked Peasbody, who had the watch.

"That water is fresh," I cried. "You are pumping the ship's drinking water overboard."

Down I went into the hold then and moved aft to where our water barrels were kept. They were stored high in a small hold of their own to keep them out of the bilges. Each barrel was held in place either by chocks or by lashings to prevent it bumping into the other in the rolling of the ship. An appalling sight greeted me as I slipped through the hatch into the hold where the barrels were stored. The whole place was strewed with barrels, their sides stove in, their contents spilled.

Not a cask had been spared, and it was plain we had not as much as ten gallons of fresh water left on board. I surveyed this wreckage, holding a lantern aloft in silence, and was interrupted by Silver thrusting his huge fair head over the hatchway to peer down at me and the chaos which had been made of our water supply.

"Well now, Tom, here's an unlucky ship if I ever saw one," he said. "Half the crew on their backs, wounds going rotten for all our care, and hardly a sip of water to pass out among the hands."

"Silver," I cried, "this is your doing!"

"Tom," said Silver, shaking his big head in reproach, "that ain't what I'd call civil. Here's me working me blessed heart out attending the sick and cooking for all hands, blow high, blow low, and there's that Captain Samuels choking on every spoonful and not seaman enough to look to his fresh water after a blow. Not civil, Tom. Not civil by a long haul."

16

WE HAD NO CHOICE now but, turning west, to run in on the Florida coast. The most careful questioning of the crew failed to reveal who had cut our water casks loose, though there was no doubt in my mind that Silver was behind it. Silver had won the greater part of the crew over to his side; such is the corruption that can be spread among men when the prospect of riches is laid before them. That same crew, which without treasure aboard would have stood by their captain and their ship in every hardship, was now utterly disaffected, looked to Silver as their leader, and some among them had the temerity to cheer the announcement that we must now head for the Florida coast.

When that course had been set, Captain Samuels summoned his officers aft and put the case clearly to us all in the privacy of his cabin.

"I have lost control of this ship in all but name," he said. "I should have kept Silver in irons from the word go, but I was persuaded against it. I accept the fault, however, for the decision was mine. We must rely on fetching St. Augustine and appealing to the Spanish authorities. I can think of nothing else. Meanwhile, let every man be on watch. St. Augustine may by no means be to Master Silver's fancy. The Tortugas or Jamaica would be more to his liking, I'm sure. I don't know whether he has corrupted my hands to the point of downright mutiny and murder, but watch behind you when you are alone on deck."

"Sir," I said, "I think you should seize Silver now. To do so would be to reassert your authority on board and to throw down a challenge to the men in clear terms. They must either follow you or follow Silver. As matters stand, they follow Silver, who has provided them with an opportunity of running contrary to your wishes without the charge of mutiny."

"Nothing would be more to my liking than to seize him and hang him this moment," said the captain. "If he were to bat his eye at the wrong moment, I would do it, but he is as cunning as a fox."

"You may seize him on suspicion," I said. "And he is, after all, a notorious pirate."

"What do you say, Mr. Peasbody?" asked the captain.

Peasbody would have preferred not to say anything, but pressed, said that it would be better to wait until we reached St. Augustine before proceeding against Silver. Mr. Hogan supported me, agreeing that Silver should be seized but it

134.

should be managed quietly and the crew informed later that he had been put in irons. We could manage it in the small hours. Hodge, the bosun, was loyal, and so was old Smigley, and perhaps one or two others, and their loyalty would be greatly heartened by seizing the man whom we all knew was disaffecting the crew and provoking one crisis after another on the brig.

It was agreed that he would be taken at two bells of the midnight watch, which is four in the morning in land time. That was Peasbody's watch, and the plan was that I would wake Silver with a pistol at his head, and Hodge to support me, and bring him aft to the main cabin, where he would be put in irons.

Alas, we had delayed too long. Shortly after midnight, when at the change of the watch I had gone to my cabin to rest for a moment or two, Hodge came crashing through the door. "They've seized Captain Samuels on deck," he cried. I reached for a cutlass hung on the bulkhead beside me, but Hodge wrenched it from my hand. "Tom," he said, "if you appear armed, you're a dead man."

"What is this?" I cried. "Are you one of them?" And seizing the cutlass again, I darted past him out the companion to the waist of the ship. I had no sooner gained the deck than I was knocked to my knees from behind by a blow of a belaying pin, overpowered, and thrust up against the butt of the mainmast, where I found the captain already tied up and his forehead drenched with blood from a blow which had felled him.

"Thank God," were his first words. "I thought you dead."

135.

Next Mr. Hogan appeared between two of the mutineers, and then Peasbody was dragged forward. He had had the watch, and whatever his weakness of character, he had done more to defend his captain and ship than I, for he had a cut across his forehead.

Silver was in command, having decided at last to show his true colors. He leaned on his crutch, a pistol in one hand, and surveyed us in silence. Catching sight of me, he cried, "Tom, don't be a fool. That's a good head you have on your shoulders. Join us and sign articles and it will be share and share alike, like jolly brothers. Resist and you'll feed the sharks."

"Silver," I said, "of fourteen jolly brothers that reached Flint's Island with you, there are only two of them now alive. Think of that, those of you who hold Silver your friend," I added, raising my voice. "That man never stopped at murder, and how many of you do you think will survive when each one killed adds to Silver's take?"

"You shut up," said Green.

"Let him say on," said Silver. "I never was afeared of lies. Not I. Fourteen he says come ashore with me at that there island. Now how would he know that, that wasn't there? And as for killing, I reckon we could all take lessons from him and Captain Samuels there. There's two was killed by treachery up in that cave, and four or five others in retaking this here ship, and then there's Calkins that died aboard of neglect. And Stennis now that will lose his arm from the same cause. And what kind of a captain is it that loses his ship twice in a month, lets wounded men die for lack of proper care, would sooner save his treasure in Savannah than save his hands here in Florida, and lost every blessed pint of fresh water that we got on board?

"This here crew's elected me captain, men having the right to save their lives. Captain Samuels is demoted. All we got to do now is decide, fair and square, what to do with him, seeing he ain't likely to join us."

"By God," cried the captain, "if you will give me a cutlass, we will decide man to man who is the best of the two of us."

"Them's brave words," said Silver, "and me that cut down seven, as they say. Long John's willing. Shall that be it, mates?" turning to the mutineers.

But I think some of them were already having second thoughts over their mutiny and hoped that if they had not the captain's death on their hands, they might, retaken, claim a measure of clemency. I sensed this uncertainty, and Mr. Hogan sensed it too, for he spoke quietly to the men, saying that they had been misled by Long John, and if they would set the captain free and return to their duty, not a hair of their heads would be hurt.

"A day or two at the latest will see us in St. Augustine," he concluded. "There the wounded can be cared for, the ship reconditioned, and we can all return to our homes."

The issue balanced on a knife edge at that moment and I think would have turned in our favor had Captain Samuels remained silent. But he was a blunt man of no tact and he burst out, saying, "Every one of you are guilty of mutiny at this moment. I command you as your captain to return

137.

to your duty." I think that one word "mutiny" cost him the ship. It stirred the men's doubts of what would happen to them when they got back to New England. Green announced that he would take his chances at fame and fortune with Long John.

"By thunder," said Silver. "There's a man worth sailing with as a gentleman of fortune." One or two others sided with Green, and so, because of the captain's lack of nicety, our cause was lost. Though Long John was in favor of death there and then, and so voted, the decision was to give us the yawl and cast us adrift.

Before I descended into the boat, Long John made one more attempt to win me over. "Tom," he said, "you're a fool. Stay on this ship, you'd have ten thousand pounds in a month. Get into that boat and you're getting into your coffin."

I said nothing, but went over the side. Only two hands joined us—Smigley, the old carpenter, who begged to be allowed his tools, and Hodge. Long John was for giving us nothing but the bare boat, but some of the others insisted that we be given a musket, two cutlasses, and a small jar of water. Just before the yawl, bobbing about in the dark water in the pool of light cast by the stern lantern, was cast off, Green appeared at the taffrail and called out, "Here's your share." He heaved one of the smaller silver ingots, weighing about thirty pounds, over the side. Had it hit the bottom of the yawl, she would have been stove there and then, and that may have been his intention. Instead, the ingot struck the gunwale and tumbled inboard. We paid it no attention.

The yawl, from the battering it had received during the gale, was leaking, and we scooped the water out as fast as we might with our hands, to the laughter and jeers of our former shipmates. Then the line was cast off, the *Jane*'s yards were trimmed, and she drew away into the dark, headed not west but southward.

"Dry Tortugas," snorted Captain Samuels, watching her go. "That's where she's headed. And the wounded hands can go hang—that's Mr. Silver for you."

17

I WILL NOT DETAIL the terrible voyage which followed in the yawl. We had thought ourselves but twenty leagues at most from the Florida coast and perhaps sixty from St. Augustine northwest of us. But when the rest of that night and the day which followed had gone by with no sign of land, we began to doubt our reckoning. While latitude may be determined by a sight of the noonday sun or of Polaris, the north star (whose elevation above the horizon gives in degrees the position of a vessel north of the equator), no method has yet been devised of establishing longitude, which is the position east or west of the Greenwich meridian.* We knew, when cast adrift, that we were off the Florida coast, and south of St. Augustine, but how

* Chronometers, from which longitude may be reckoned, weren't available generally at this time. *Editor*

many miles off was a matter of guesswork, obscured by our drift during the storm.

Our greatest suffering was occasioned by the sun, which for twelve hours a day beat down upon us without mercy. We set the two lugsails of the yawl, and only in the forenoon and afternoon could we have some shade from them, as well as drive. But in the greatest heat of the day, the sun being almost directly overhead, hardly a scrap of shade was afforded us. Mr. Hogan suffered the most. His chest wound became inflamed, red as a boil, and he complained on the second day of swellings in his armpits. Captain Samuels, who had a scalp wound from the blow which felled him in mutiny, examined Mr. Hogan and said his wound needed cauterizing, but we had no means of achieving this. The captain undertook, however, to lance it with a knife when a quantity of watery blood exuded. The only other treatment was to wash the wound constantly in sea water, and under this treatment there was some improvement, so that in three days the swellings under the arms were reduced, and Mr. Hogan, though feverish, was able to sit up for a while in the boat.

The long boat, or yawl, was carvel-built—that is to say, her planks were laid edge to edge rather than overlapping— and this was the saving of us. The rough treatment she had endured during the gale had loosened her fastenings, but we made caulking by teasing out her rope painter, and Smigley, by pulling out nails here and there which he judged superfluous, was able to refasten her in some kind. True, he grumbled all the while that it was not a proper

141.

job and would all have to be done again, and it was surprising how comforting it was to hear him grumble, as if he were aboard the *Jane* instead of cast adrift in a thirty-foot boat. His main complaint against Silver and the mutineers was that they had hustled him into the yawl without letting him get a favorite saw which he always kept, wrapped in green baize cloth, on a rack beside his bunk.

"Sheffield made, it were," he said, "and belonged to my own father, and now it will just hang there and rust, or some fool will get it that won't know how to set the teeth, and will ruin it forever."

"Mr. Smigley," said Captain Samuels, "upon my honor I will get you the finest saw obtainable when we are safely home."

"Thank you kindly," said Smigley, "but I'll be afeared for that saw to my dying day."

On the second night out the yawl ran into a series of heavy squalls which nearly swamped us, both from shipping seas and from the deluge of the rain. The rain poured down in torrents and we bailed with our hands, and indeed with our arms, for all our worth. Several seas came over the stern, and after a fearful night Smigley took out one of the thwarts, or seats, and, splitting it carefully with an ax, began to contrive weather cloths to put about our stern to keep out the sea in rough weather. We owed a great deal to Smigley. Grumble he did, for it was as natural to him as breathing. Yet with almost no wood, and having to hunt for and deliberate over every nail he used, he had contrived the weather cloths for us and then made a bailer out of the top of his tool chest, which he cut up and fashioned into a four-sided bucket.

The weather cloths were made of the smaller of our lugsails, and with the canvas left over and a few sticks from the rest of the tool-chest top, Smigley made a cone-shaped container with a wooden lip, which we used for catching rain water. Although the water caught was brackish from sluicing down our remaining sail, yet it was drinkable and allayed our thirst.

We had not as much as a ship's biscuit on board in the way of food, or a hook or line with which to fish. On the third day Hodge pointed to a shark cruising astern of us, and the menace of that fin was with us through the whole of that miserable voyage. On the fourth day, I think, in the evening, when Captain Samuels had led us in prayer, we heard a great deal of fluttering in the bow of the yawl and found a flying fish there, weighing about a pound and a half. It was divided among the five of us—the first nourishment we had had since leaving the *Jane*—and it was eaten entrails and all. Nothing before or since ever tasted so delicious, and although it is the fashion these days to mock at the Providence of God, yet it seemed to me then, and does now that our earnest prayers for help (should we be thought deserving of it) had been heard by our Heavenly Father.

That fish brought a change in our fortunes. Toward noon of the fifth day Hodge, who was then at the tiller, sighted a dot of land on the western horizon, and although for several terrible minutes none of the rest of us could see it, land it proved to be and no more than ten miles off. We had an onshore wind and were a few hundred yards off the barrier reef, which is to be found along the greater part of that coast, well before evening. Beyond the reef lay a beach of dirty-looking sand with behind it many of those same kind of pines we had found on Flint's Island.

For two anxious hours we pulled on the oars, skirting the reef, before we found a reasonable passage through to the mouth of a small, muddy river. Once through the passage and in the lagoon beyond, we turned the boat's head ashore and, instead of beaching her, took her a little distance up the mouth of the stream for concealment and tied her to a tree by the bank. We got out painfully, as cramped as crabs whose shells have been cracked. For myself, I found I could scarcely keep my balance from vertigo brought on by weakness and hunger, and Mr. Hogan went ashore on all fours, as it were, and lay for a while on his back, the world, as he said, reeling about him.

When we had caught our breath and our balance, we took the sail ashore and rigged a shelter and brought ashore Smigley's tool chest, the musket and cutlasses. It was Hodge who remembered the ingot of silver and, picking it up, carried it inside our little tent and put it down before Captain Samuels. Black with tarnish, it still had that deep velvet gleam which we had noted in the cave on Flint's Island. Captain Samuels eyed it in silence and then said, "Had we a mold, we could make capital bullets out of that."

That day, being uncertain of where we might be—whether in Spanish territory or in a place where the Indian tribes were hostile to invaders—Captain Samuels would not permit a musket to be fired, even though, exploring in the marsh about the river, Hodge and I came upon flocks of wild fowl. However, we found in the mud in the marsh and estuary of the river vast beds of oysters and others of large clams, though the clams preferred a sandy berth. These, boiled, provided a rich and nourishing meal and soon restored our strength.

We stayed in this place two days, recovering from our sea ordeal, and then the captain pointing out that we could travel better by sea than by land and would be more proof against surprise in the boat, we took the yawl and went up the coast in the quiet water which lay behind the coral reef.

When we had gone perhaps twenty miles, we came on a small hut on the beach, under the shade of a grove of pines. It proved old and empty. Farther on, we found two other buildings which had been burned to the ground, though many years before, for creepers were growing all over them. In the afternoon we passed several islets offshore to the east, while inland the terrain turned to vast swamps out of which grew great snarled trees, draped with moss like gravecloths. We thought ourselves deep in the wilds of the Floridas. Imagine, then, our surprise when, rounding the point of one large and hilly island, expecting to see ahead a further dismal prospect of swamp and gnarled trees, we came instead upon a settlement of good houses, some with gardens about them and washing hanging on lines to dry in the sun. There was a jetty of good size by the shore, and we pulled in here in wonder—a boatload of scarecrows dumped right in the middle of what might have been, to judge by appearances, a New England village. The greatest number of those who crowded down to the jetty at our approach were blacks, however, but there were several whites among them, and one of these, in a fine blue coat with yellow facings, pushed to the fore.

"Ahoy the boat," he yelled. "Who are you?"

"Captain Edward Samuels, brig *Jane* out of Salem," was the reply. "May I be informed, sir, what place is this?"

"Port of Marystown, His Britannic Majesty's colony of Georgia," was the reply.

At that a ragged little cheer went up from our boat, in which even old Smigley joined, for we were within the king's dominions, and safe at last.

18

WE WERE THE heroes of Marystown as soon as we stepped ashore, and nothing was held back for our comfort that the town and its people could provide. A house, recently vacated, was placed at our disposal, and a doctor summoned immediately to attend to Mr. Hogan—Peasbody's and the captain's scalp wound being now all but healed. Quite half of the whites in the town were German, many having settled in Georgia under the great Oglethorpe to avoid religious persecution in their own country.

Dr. Weiger was one of these—a sparse, small man, gentle in his ways, and given to reflection. "Blut poison," he said quietly as soon as he saw Mr. Hogan's wound, and without fuss set about the horrid business of cauterizing the whole length of it with hot knives. Brutal as the treatment was, it worked wonders for our sailing master, whose major worry was that he should be available when a ship was found and fitted to search out Long John Silver in the *Jane*.

That, of course, was Captain Samuels's chief concern. Indeed, such was his haste that the day after our arrival, when our story had been told in full to the town officials, he had made arrangements to travel to Savannah and there beg the use of a colonial vessel with which to hunt down Silver. A sloop of war, the *Hornet*, was promised and fitted out in such short order that the people of Marystown were surprised at the alacrity of the governor and thought the treasure aboard the *Jane* might provide the explanation here. The people of Marystown were annoyed too, for, being at the time the closest settlement to the Spanish lands, which lay but a few miles to the south, they had often asked that they be provided with a small war vessel for their protection, but none had been afforded them.

"Treasure talks," said Mr. Wedcock, voicing the opinion of all. Mr. Wedcock, the same gentleman in the blue coat and yellow facings who had greeted us on arrival, was mayor of the town, though the title is too large for so small a place. "Treasure talks. And Flint's treasure talks louder in Savannah, I would say, than anywhere else in the world." Well it might, indeed, for Flint had found a kind of welcome in Savannah, for the curious reason that so notorious a pirate, cruising the Georgia coast, was a strong deterrent to Spanish attack, which was always uppermost in the minds of the colonists. Some (who did not know him) thought Flint something of a patriot in that most of the treasure he took came from the Spanish possessions, though no ship at sea was safe from Flint. Savannah, Flint never attacked, even pirates, I suppose, needing a home port, and it was off Savannah, as I have said, that he died of a thundering stroke while deep in rum.

Three weeks after he had left us to go to Savannah, Captain Samuels returned with the colonial vessel *Hornet*, mounting four eight-pounders and, though rated as a sloop of war, schooner-rigged. His only major trouble was in the enlisting of a crew, for although everybody wanted a share of Flint's hoard, not many, when it came to signing, were prepared to risk an encounter with Flint's hands. Peasbody, who had been very much the hero with the cutlass stroke he had received in the mutiny, volunteered immediately, and it was a surprise to me to find such stout courage in a man of such meanness of mind. I volunteered, of course, and so did Hodge and Smigley—Smigley, I am sure, with the hope of getting back that treasured saw of his, which he envisioned worsening each day in its baize cloth over his berth. Mr. Hogan insisted that he should be allowed to come, though Dr. Weiger was opposed.

"You go perhaps to your death," he said solemnly, and Mr. Hogan asked quietly whether it was not to their death that all men went, day by day. To our surprise, the thoughtful German doctor himself volunteered, and we were glad of his services, which, should we meet the *Jane*, would certainly be required.

A month, then, after our arrival in Marystown, the *Hornet* slipped out to sea, myself with a second mate's post, and Hodge, formerly our bosun, filling the offices both of quartermaster and of gunnery officer. "Small ships, big berths," he said. "I'd make captain in a bumboat."

We had been warned by Mr. Wedcock to stay clear of St. Augustine, which I was surprised to learn was the oldest settlement on the American main, outdating even Plymouth and Boston by many years. "The Spanish, sir, are no more to be trusted than your man Silver himself. They will cut your throat while offering you a glass of wine. You will find, sir, that deceit and Romanism go hand in hand in these parts."

But Dr. Weiger, staunch Protestant though he was, held another view. "You may trust the Spanish if you go plainly to them," he said. "They will honor a flag of truce, and news of every ship that touches the coast of Florida is eventually reported there. A month has gone by since the mutiny, and perhaps the Spanish already have some news of the *Jane*."

So it was that, once at sea, we ignored Mr. Wedcock's jaundiced view and, touching at St. Augustine, learned that Indians, widely used as an intelligence service, had reported a large vessel which had put in at Sand Cape on the southern tip of Florida, where a dead man had been buried ashore and water taken aboard. This could certainly be no other vessel than the *Jane*, and the man who died likely poor Stennis with his gangrened arm. We left St. Augustine immediately on receiving this news, and with a following wind we plunged southward to Sand Cape.

The *Hornet*, schooner-rigged, sailed but poorly before

the wind, and yet it was a delight to me to have a deck under my feet again and feel the lift and roll of the little sloop of war as she staggered southward. The wind went into the northwest when we rounded the tip of Florida, and here the *Hornet* showed her mettle, plunging along like a good horse that has found its stride, an acre of foam under her leeward rail as she reeled off the knots.

We put in at Sand Cape, meeting there some Indians clad in tatters of clothing and one wearing a seaman's belt which Hodge recognized as having belonged to Stennis. These unfortunates begged for food and tobacco, and in return, one who answered to the surprising name of Andrew volunteered the information that the ship whose captain had but one leg had gone off in the direction of the Florida keys —that long chain of islets which extends many miles into the Caribbean Sea from the end of Florida.

Off we went then, and began a search of the keys, putting in at every islet and exploring every cove. The small size of our schooner was an advantage in threading the tortuous channels through coral which bestrewed the lovely green and blue waters of the keys. From a landsman's point of view, there is surely no lovelier place in the world than this region, with its islets of glittering sand, its waters of light emerald and deepest blue, with here and there a fringe of palms rustling against the sky. But for a seaman these waters are a nightmare, the coral so thick and the channels through so narrow and twisting that a moment's hesitation at the helm, or a correction wrongly applied, could mean disaster.

151.

Charts were useless for work among the coral. We had our best hands at the masthead all through the day and were constrained to anchor at night. And so we went from islet to islet, inspecting every likely cove and sending our boats ashore to explore the larger islets for any clues to the *Jane*. A few Indians lived on these islands, and one or two whites and blacks who had turned their backs on their own world. They insisted they knew nothing of the *Jane*, but a present of good London snuff (which the Indians of these parts prefer to plain tobacco) produced the vague news that a brig had passed, but nothing further.

At last, on one of the keys known as Pine Island, we learned that a white man had come ashore on an island nearby and was hiding there from the brig, which he had deserted. And when we had put our boats ashore on the island, who should come running down the beach, hallooing with all his might, but Green, who had been foremost among the hands in the mutiny. You may imagine how he looked when he found himself confronted by Captain Samuels and myself. His face, in the tropical sun, went a shade paler; his jaw dropped, and I fancy he could see the hangman's noose dangling before him.

"Well, Green," said the captain, arms akimbo, eyeing the young sailor. "First mutiny and then desertion. You've some curious ways for a seaman."

"Sir," said Green, "mutiny is a fair charge. But desertion I deny, for I have only returned to my duty."

His story was soon told and gave the greatest satisfaction to Captain Samuels. Green had expected that after the

152.

mutiny, having supported Silver, he would become one of the *Jane*'s officers. But, instead, Silver had promoted his two surviving cronies over the *Jane*'s crew, and these, between hazing the crew, threats of death, and bouts of drunkenness, had utterly demoralized the men, who were heartily sick of the voyage and only remained aboard in hope of their share of the treasure.

"I slipped ashore a week ago and have been hiding ever since, for Silver laid it down that only dead men leave his ship, being afraid of informers," said Green. "If I am to be hung, so be it. But I'd sooner hanging than a life among Silver and his blackguards."

"And where is my ship now?" demanded Captain Samuels.

"She was headed for Hispaniola but was to stop at Shark Island," said Green.

"Shark Island," said Captain Samuels, "now there's a strange port of call. It is nothing more than a sandspit where turtles lay their eggs. There's nothing there but a brackish lagoon and a little mangrove in the way of wood and water. Why would he want to call at Shark Island?"

"Why," said Mr. Hogan, "what Flint did once, Silver can do again, I suppose. They both learned out of the same book. Buccaneers, having a great want of bankers, are driven to bury their hoards. It is my opinion that Silver intends to bury the treasure on Shark Island, saving out what he needs for the next few years, and killing off the witnesses. Flint did the same on his island, using one of the dead as a marker, as Silver himself told us. Silver, I would

153.

say, is a good scholar and will follow Flint's example."

"If Silver and the other two kill what is left of the *Jane*'s crew," said the captain, "how can he handle the brig thereafter?"

"Sir," said Mr. Hogan, "he would not have far to go, by my reckoning. Three at a pinch could handle her the thirty miles across the channel to Hispaniola. If three is too much company for Master Silver, I fancy he could pistol his companions in midchannel, burn the brig, and make the rest of the way in a small boat alone. Undoubtedly he has replaced the ship's boats and must have at least a gig for his service. Silver has powerful shoulders—an advantage, as he once pointed out, derived from having lost his leg. A few miles with oars would be no great task for Silver. That's his plan, I fancy. Or something like it."

The prospect of his ship being burned spurred Captain Samuels to even greater effort. He took Green on board and set sail immediately for Shark Island, ignoring all the islands between. The unfortunate Green was put in irons and confined in a horrid dark hole aft for the next twenty-four hours. The excessive heat below decks, and the galls which the irons quickly wore into his wrists and ankles, turned what was designed as confinement into torture. Dr. Weiger protested the treatment, and the general feeling was that Green was more weak than wicked. So he was set free, to be chained again when we reached port, when he must stand trial for his life. In the days that followed, he became a good friend of our German doctor, who, I think, pitied Green for his youth.

154.

We made Shark Island in the forenoon of the following day. It presented a curious sight—a tangle of mangroves growing, it seemed, out of the middle of the ocean, with a number of taller pines, the seeding of birds, overtopping them. We crowded forward to view it, and then there came an excited hail from the lookout perched like a bird on the jaws of the foresail gaff. "A sail beyond the island," he cried. "Looks like a small brig. Headed southeast."

"Clap the topsails on her," cried Captain Samuels, for this was the moment he had been waiting for. "Mr. Whelan, break out that Genoese jib and the fisherman's staysail. Mr. Hodge, cutlasses to all hands, if you please. I want one round from those eight-pounders at pistol range and then we'll board. We'll take her to weather."

The *Jane*, for such indeed the little brig proved to be, was not being well sailed. She was reaching for Hispaniola, with her yards out of trim, so that our lookout reported her topsails luffing, then filling and luffing again.

To remain concealed, we kept Shark Island between us and the brig as long as we might, and when we at last had to slip past the island and into view, the brig—so badly handled, and without a lookout, it seemed—was but four miles off. I think it was only then that she spotted us, and the chase was on.

On a broad reach, the *Hornet* was faster than the *Jane*, and so we came down on her handsomely. But the *Jane* put down her wheel and trimmed her yards better to run before the wind, which, being the best point of sailing for a square-rigger and the worst for a schooner, she was soon drawing

155.

away from us. To add to our difficulties, the weather now turned squally, as is often the case in the neighborhood of islands like Hispaniola. Twice the *Jane*, which had now increased her lead to five miles, was lost to us in the deluge of rain that always accompanies such squalls. She was moving far faster than we and, with the aid of squalls, was soon but a white dot on the horizon and the chase seemed lost.

The *Hornet* could not flee before the following wind like the *Jane*, and we had to take in our topsail or lose our spars, though, even in the worst of the squalls, we kept the big Genoese-cut jib out boomed overboard to weather. After the last black squall had passed over the *Jane*, she was not to be seen at all, and we thought her over the horizon from us. Then the lookout raised a shout of triumph. "There she is," he cried. "Dead to leeward. She's lost her topmasts. I see her plain and she has but lowers and courses set."

"She's ours," cried Captain Samuels. "How is the powder, Mr. Hodge? Not damp, I trust."

"Dry as a bone," said Hodge. "I made up the cartridges myself."

Just then a shot whistled over the *Hornet* and plunged into the water astern. The captain eyed the fall of the shot calmly, and said, "Silver will expect us to fall off. A touch to windward, helmsman, if you please." Sure enough, the schooner having been put half a point closer to the wind, the next shot fell a hundred yards to leeward, as Captain Samuels had guessed. It was quickly followed by another, which fell so close that the splash came up on our decks and brought from Captain Samuels the remark that Flint had always had notable gunners.

After that, the brig fell a little off the wind herself, though we had not ourselves fired. There was plainly something aboard which had engaged the attention of her helmsman. She tended to round up to the wind and then, the luff of her sails shivering, fall away again. One more squall passed over us and then over her and the brig disappeared once again in the purple torrent of rain. Then, from the depths of the squall, came a heavy detonation and a lurid yellow flash, which I thought to be lightning. The squall cleared, but the brig was nowhere to be seen. A puff of dirty yellow smoke clung to the surface of the ocean, and nothing more.

"By thunder," cried Captain Samuels. "He's blown her up."

"There's something beyond," cried the lookout. "A boat. A boat with a man, maybe more, aboard."

"Silver," cried Captain Samuels. "He'll not escape me now."

Yet escape he did. A boat the size of a gig is no great object in the ocean. We were looking for Silver in the full light of the declining sun and the glitter of the sea. He had been three miles off when the brig was blown up, and the lookout, with glittering white caps all around, could not keep the gig in view. He lost it in the troughs of the waves, and though we searched about until sunset, we found no further trace of the boat. Reluctantly then we set our course for Shark Island, passing through the debris of the *Jane* as we did so. Old Smigley eyed the few small pieces sadly, thinking no doubt of that fine saw of his which he would never see again.

19

FLINT'S HOARD HAD gone down with the *Jane*, less whatever considerable portion of it Long John had been able to load into the boat. Whether he had his two rogues with him or whether he had killed them before getting away from the brig, we did not know. Certainly he was not a man to hesitate over killing two of his fellows to increase his own profit, and one of the men, Dick, was minus a hand and so would be of little use taking the boat to Hispaniola.

We had been wrong in assuming that Long John intended to bury the treasure on Shark Island. When we reached that miserable sandspit with its few straggly pines and its stinking wreath of mangrove, we found there what remained of the *Jane*'s crew—half a dozen men, unarmed, three of them still suffering from wounds, and all marooned by Silver.

"More of the Jolly Brethren of the Coast," said Captain Samuels when we found them. "Ship gone. Treasure gone. You paid a high price for your mutiny, didn't you? And every one of you that's sound with your neck in a noose."

From start to finish, Silver had played a winning hand. He had duped Captain Samuels on Flint's Island until all the treasure was aboard, when he had struck. Foiled there, and once at sea, he had duped the crew into mutiny, and then he had duped them again, deserting them on Shark Island while he went off with his two fellows, who, I believe, he had disposed of in midchannel. Thinking back on the whole story, from the moment Mr. Arrow had been killed, I saw that Silver had had the upper hand, his greatest weapon being neither pistol nor cutlass but his ability to play a part, putting such a color of plain honesty into his manner that I think that, brought to court, he would have deceived a bench of magistrates.

The poor wretches on Shark Island were only too glad to be taken off, despite the fate that likely lay ahead for the three among them who were unwounded, for the others of course had not had any hand in the mutiny. They could give no defense for their actions but a few muttered phrases about caring for the wounded, being short of water, and Silver's powers of persuasion, which had initially deceived even Captain Samuels. The captain was as hard as iron toward them. Mutiny was mutiny, and on that charge—a capital one, you may be sure—he intended they should be

160.

tried at the earliest moment. Two were from families neighbor to my own in Salem, and all came from good New England homes. But when I mentioned this to Captain Samuels, he was all the more hard against them. "Good families," he snorted. "All the more reason why they should have stood by their captain and their ship. They shall hang, every one of them. If they are spared, roguery everywhere will be encouraged and no ship safe at sea."

So Green and the three others were put on trial as soon as we reached Savannah. I think they would all have been hanged indeed, but for Dr. Weiger, who, as I have said, had conceived a great liking for Green. He hired a lawyer for their defense, and that gentleman, I believe, was the only man I have met who might have outfoxed Long John Silver. He allowed the trial to proceed until a verdict of guilty had been returned. He then rose to question not the verdict but the legality of the whole proceeding, saying that the defendants, facing a capital charge, had the right to trial in England; that they had not been made aware of that right; that they likewise had a right to trial by their peers, and gentlemen resident in Georgia and the masters of several hundred pounds a year could not claim to be the peers of New England fishermen forced by hardship to earn their living on the high seas. In fact, he cast such a vast shadow of doubt over the whole trial that in the end a mistrial was declared, the court was bedeviled and bullied into ruling that it had no jurisdiction, and the case sent to be tried again in Boston or in London.

I will not weary you with the maze of legalities which

Dr. Weiger's lawyer was able to stir up—varying from the payment of the prisoners' costs in transporting them from Savannah to Boston or to London (a charge, he said, which must be met out of the revenues of Georgia) to a demand that Silver be produced in court as a witness on behalf of the prisoners. I have earlier remarked on the distrust that seamen, unlettered, entertain for lawyers, and how Silver, playing on this, had encouraged the men to mutiny lest they be robbed of their share of the treasure in Boston. The men now had an example of legal gymnastics, operating not against them but entirely in their favor. They were all taken to Boston and made to stand trial there. But that trial also resulted in a mistrial, the same lawyer arguing that under the English system no man might twice be put in jeopardy of his life on the same charge.

"These men have already undergone the ordeal of trial in Savannah, Georgia," said the lawyer smoothly. "Are they now to have to undergo trial on the same charge in Boston? And then perhaps again in London? Is this the kind of justice England affords her colonists, expanding her commerce on the seas?" Boston was, of course, of all places, a sailors' town, and the current of feeling at the time ran heavily against England. The upshot of this man's performance was that the case was thrown out of court and the men became unwilling heroes of the Boston mob for a day or two and then quietly returned to their homes. This outcome, I thought, provided far more of an object lesson in the futility of mutiny than had they been hanged. They had gained

162.

nothing whatever by their rebellion, which, on the contrary, had cost them their chance at a fortune.

Our total take from all that treasure in the cave and in the four chests of jewels amounted but to the one silver ingot, which Green in derision had flung into the yawl when we were cast adrift. My own share of this, when title was established and it had been weighed and sold and divided, amounted to two and a half sovereigns.

The day I got payment, I put the small gold pieces on the table before my mother and my little brothers and sisters, who thought me a very great hero and never tired of my telling them the story. "Pirate gold," I said. "You wanted to see some, and there it is. Captain Samuels was quite right when he said he never knew of any good to come of treasure."

"We have you safely home, Tom. It is all the treasure we need," my mother said. "Had you been lost, a house full of jewels could not have taken your place." She picked the gold pieces up and put them in a little wooden tea caddy we had from China—one of the most cherished possessions of our household. "We don't need that money now," she said. "Later we may find some very good use for it."

So it all seemed over and done with, and the money might have been spent on a score of domestic needs had I not one day met old Mr. Tedguard, who was the sexton at the church in Salem. He was a kindly man, knew of the needs of my family, and took some interest in us.

"Young Whelan," he said, "if you want a piece of land

to graze a goat, I have a bargain for you, right here in this town. It is that same plot where that old villain of a pirate is buried. Not a soul has been buried anywhere near there since that day, and the parish is to sell the land about off. It will go for thirty shillings—a third of an acre, and good grazing."

"Then I'll buy it," I said, and the bargain was struck. My mother was delighted and got the money out of the tea caddy to make the purchase, having enough over for two female goats, one of them in kid. Some weeks later Captain Samuels stopped by at the house with talk of a new command and asked me whether I would take a berth as second with him. He stayed for dinner and I mentioned how I had bought at a bargain the land where Flint had once buried one of his crew, and so had something to show for all our adventures.

"Flint," said Captain Samuels slowly. "That man, I think, was the very devil in human form. I don't think I was ever so stirred to horror in all my life as at the story of the sea-man's bones he used as a marker to point the way to his hoard. Even the dead were tools for Flint."

That phrase "the dead were tools for Flint" struck home immediately with me. I recalled my father's story of that mockery of a funeral which Flint had held at pistol point on that very piece of land which now belonged to me, and this, coupled with the tale of the skeleton used as a marker, took on, suddenly, a tremendous significance. I leaped up from the table overwhelmed by my thoughts, and cried, "Captain, come with me," and dashed from the room.

"Where are you going?" he cried.

"We are going to dig up a grave," I replied. I got mattocks, shovels, and lanterns from our little toolshed, and we had soon located the grave where the body had been put down twenty years before. It being the fall of the year, the ground was soft, and I was able in an hour's brisk work to drive a shaft down to the horrid earth-stained sailcloth six feet below the ground. My hands trembling, I turned the spade on edge and drove it into the canvas. I half expected some revolting softness, but instead the edge of the spade struck something rock hard which gave off a metallic clink. I jumped into the shaft I had made, ripped the rotted canvas aside, and stooping picked up a handful of coins and a necklace set with bright stones, which I held up in the light of the lantern to Captain Samuels.

"Flint's way," I cried. "You were right. He used the dead as tools, and what better bank for a man like Flint than a grave in a Christian cemetery?"

I have come now to the end of my tale. The treasure was valued, in English sterling, at a hundred thousand pounds. Close to a tenth of that sum was spent in legal fees establishing my title to it. One-third went to the Crown as Treasure Trove. There was still more than I, my mother, and my little brothers and sisters could spend for the rest of our lives, and after discussing it with them, we agreed that we would share it with all of the *Jane*'s crew who had been loyal to the end or the dependents of those who had not survived. Though Captain Samuels protested, my mother would not have it any other way, and indeed there were still riches for all. The treasure shared out, I bought a bigger house for my family, and hired a servant to help my mother, and so we are set up very comfortably indeed.

I, however, continued to go to sea. I knew that a life of leisure or a venture into politics (both now at my disposal) might well be the ruin of me. To complete my tale, I have only to add that Captain Samuels was as good as his word and obtained for Smigley as fine a saw as was ever made in Sheffield. When it was presented to the dour old ship's carpenter at a little gathering at the Blue Anchor in Salem, he acknowledged it a fine tool, thanked the captain, and immediately mourned the loss of those chests of oak in which the treasure on Flint's Island had been contained.

"We'll never see the like again," he said, and though Silver perhaps got away with one or two of them, I hold that a true word indeed.